BEFORE THE FIRST DAY

by

STEPHEN M. HALE

xulon PRESS

Before the First Day
by Stephen M. Hale

Printed in the United States of America

ISBN 9781628391343

Unless otherwise indicated, Bible quotations are taken from the King James Version.

www.xulonpress.com

Pastor Denis -

Thank You for your Dedication to our Lord & Creator.. And for being His mouthpiece to us more times than I can count. Truly you are becoming the Semsa that He Saw in you long ago. May you Touch others that He Leads to you, continuing to strengthen the Army of the Lord... Lead by Semsas.

Blessings to you and your Family.

In ∞

Steve Vale

DEDICATION

This book is dedicated to my Dad and Mom, Gerard & Jeanette Hale.

Dad, I know you're with Jesus now and seeing things now far better than our best stereoscope and digital sound could provide. I just wanted you to know that I forever am grateful for the time when I was little that you took us to the drive-in to see what you thought was *The Preacher from the Black Lagoon* but turned out to be *The Creature from the Black Lagoon* instead. The dreams (and nightmares) that followed became something else He intended me to use later.

Mom, you're keeping Dad company now, so you've also got "the best seats in the house." So, for all those stories you used to tell me when we were travelling… They did far more than help me keep from getting car-sick. They gave me the eyes to see the dreams and nightmares in a positive way and to imagine what I could have done if I had really been there in them. Little did you know…

I would also like to give special acknowledgement to other people who were hand-picked by the Maker to be in my life and make this come into being. I am sure this list will grow as the time goes on; however, as of this date, I offer my sincerest heartfelt praise to my Lord and King for His placing in my life:

Judith, my wife, who is also with Jesus and singing in His choir I am sure—for bringing life back into me when all I thought was death and for helping me see things with better eyes. Because of your unwavering faith in our Maker and in me, I was able to again dare to allow my heart to hear His Words and then try to put them onto parchment. And… thank you for constantly reminding me to get out of the box before I tried to decide what I was looking at.

Jewel, my wife, who is now also with Jesus, for putting up with me through my initial Spiritual evolution and the uncounted hours you spent watching me pour over the keyboard and then grabbing your magic red pen and proofing my work before I dared send it out to be edited.

Grandma, who is also with Jesus, who oftentimes didn't understand what I was doing but always told me it didn't matter whether or not anyone understood, and that I could do anything that I really wanted to.

Janet, who is also with Jesus—you were my most knowledgeable and devoted Sunday School teacher—who looked at me, saw my desire and the Words of God written on the tablets of my heart and told me to "Write—now, and let nothing stand in your way."

Luanne, my Mirror-holder of the Maker, my Compass, who reached into my darkness and rather than judge or merely offer to light a candle, wisely listened to the Words of the Maker on her own heart and told me to "breathe in, breathe out...keep doing that and everything else will work out."

Pammy, my forever friend, Truth-speaker, and encourager. You listened to His Words and to your heart and then spoke in Love and Wisdom beyond your years, bidding me go on when I felt I had let my Maker down. If not for your words, these words would never have been.

I

Prologue

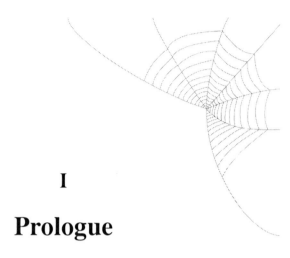

Long ago on the Earth before there were Men, before the valley became a Valley, before there were Great Ones, before there was anything to notice all that had been Made, the Sun Sang. And He Sang His Song to all that had been Made. It was a beautiful Song. It was about warmth, life, and nourishment. The Song found its way into every aspect of the world. It wound its way into the delicate spirals of the clouds. It reached into the mud in the deepest parts of the ocean floors. It crept into the tiny cracks in the mighty rocks at the bases of the hills. It burrowed through all the terrain it touched and met itself in the vast underground caverns. It coursed through the mighty River, sending life into all other rivers in other parts of the world. And everywhere it went, life came; and all that had life grew and reached up toward the Sun because of His Song.

But it was a lonely Song. It could only be Sung in the place that it was. And there was a part of the world that was not seeing Him or hearing His Song because that part was in darkness. And the Sun Longed for all to hear His Song.

So a Moon came to be in the night sky. He reflected the light of the Sun and repeated His Song. And because it was only a reflection, it was not as bright; and a second Moon came to be in the night sky, so the Song rang on, even while those beneath the Moons slept. The Moons were always careful to reflect the Sun's light exactly as He had Shown it and to sing His Song exactly as He had Sung it.

And all that lived and breathed and grew received of the Song and thrived and multiplied within their own Families.

But there came a time when the second Moon noticed that, despite all his beauty and talent, all that lived and thrived on the earth were not doing so because of <u>his</u> light or by <u>his</u> song, for he was only repeating what the Sun Sang. Moreover, he noticed that the first Moon did not seem to mind this. He began to grow discontent. He felt he did not need any help in singing the Sun's Song. He had been Given a beautiful voice or he would not be able to repeat the Song of the Sun so well. For that matter, he should be able to sing on his own. He was not content to sing the Song of the Sun, or to lead others in the singing of it. He wanted to sing his own song. He wanted to lead others in the singing of his own song.

And he purposed in his heart to do so.

He looked to the stars that also shared his sky and many of them agreed with him because of his beauty and the melodious works that came from him. Others did not, and discord grew among the stars; and for a time, there was chaos in the heavens.

One star in particular refused to listen to the unharmony now being sung by the second Moon. It knew in its heart that its life was Made and Perfected by the Sun, even though it was far, far away. It knew in the very outer layers of its blinding skin that it would soon be Called to a Purpose of which the second Moon could now never be a part. This star then patiently waited for the Call of its Name when it would feel the loving hands of the Sun Himself Ignite its inner core so that it might fulfill its Purpose.

But the second Moon knew which of them wanted him to shine his own light and sing his own song.

The day came when the laws of the created worlds dictated that a special event take place involving several of the worlds as they spun on their specially created paths in the whole of space. It was time for the first Moon to move in front of the Sun, causing a great shadow to fall over the world below it and letting the Sun's light encircle Him so that all who listened to the Song might hear a melody being Sung by Them together. And so He did.

And during that Time of Darkness, envy burned inside the second Moon, and he moved against the laws of the created worlds—against the ways he had been Shown to move—and so placed himself between the first Moon and the Earth, blocking the Melody being Sung. And he tried to sing his own song.

And there was war in heaven.

The Sun became very angry and His own Song changed from one of life to one of death. The first Moon moved out of the way and the Sun's new *Song rained down* upon the second Moon whose own song became as nothing beside that of the Sun. His own light dwindled to less than that of a star. And his insides began to hurt in the fierceness of that fiery *Song*. Anger burned within him and he tried to turn and sing his own song of death back at the Sun. It was then that he realized his pitiful state, that he had no song of his own, no song of death, not even one of life, warmth, and light. He could only reflect and repeat what the Sun was Giving him. Anger raged throughout his every fiber and he turned, determined to reflect that *Song of death* on toward the Earth.

The Sun's anger grew fiercer still and He *Directed His Song* at this Moon, Singing it louder and louder until the sky could no longer hold him. And the second Moon called for help to the stars that had agreed with him, but they turned away from the fierceness of the Sun's *Song*.

And the second Moon died. As he did, he broke into pieces under the *Song* and the pieces fell from their position of majesty in the sky. And as he died, he vowed revenge upon the Sun Who had Caused this to happen to him. He vowed revenge upon His stars and upon the first Moon Who had allowed it to happen. And he vowed revenge upon the Earth for not recognizing his own majesty and preferring it apart from the Sun's. And out of his center of death, evil, and perversion came a great Blackness, a Blackness so dark that even the light from the Sun did not go through it. The life of that Moon lived in the Blackness and looked at the pieces of his once beautiful body becoming enshrouded in flames as they plummeted toward the Earth. The Blackness smiled, for he would have part of his revenge now.

And the Sun Moved and *Sang a new Song*, and the stars that had agreed with that Moon were pulled from their places in the sky and began to fall toward the Blackness. Fissures appeared in places on the surface of the Earth, causing hills to become mountains and some valleys to become Valleys. The Earth was carefully turned under the *Song* and the fiery pieces of the dead Moon struck only the lifeless parts of the Earth, making them even more lifeless, leaving wherever they struck huge ruptures that carried embedded deeply in them the story of how this Moon had turned against the Sun, its Maker.

But the River continued to flow through those lands unbothered, carrying restoration and life to all parts of the Earth.

The Blackness burned with anger anew at the Sun and vowed his revenge on the Earth still, that he would unMake all that had been Made. So a rip, a tearing of the sky appeared near him, and out of it came nothing, for there was nothing there. The nothing expanded in size until it was big as the Blackness and his stars. And then it grew even larger and engulfed them—and was no longer empty. The Blackness and his stars screamed their vows of revenge as this *Song of the Sun grew louder and overcame* their noise. The hole in the sky closed then, leaving no sign that there had ever been anything discordant in the heavens.

The Sun and Moon Lived then in the sky with all the remaining stars. And the sky was beautiful and at peace once again.

But the Sun Knew that the Blackness would eventually come back, for the will of that Moon had been very strong. And He Knew that he would seek the revenge he had vowed upon the Earth. So the Sun Looked out into the vastness of space, now at peace, and Called the

Name of the particular star who had so strongly resisted the temptings of the second Moon.

At once the inner core of that star swelled as Commanded and erupted, sending out arms of purposeful and loving radiant energy that engulfed all that circled the star, and the light of that star then burned brighter than any in the heavens, its light being now Directed toward the Earth, to arrive and be seen at a Chosen Time signaling the Love that burned within the Sun for the Earth and all that lived thereon.

And the Sun Purposed in His heart to Place a guard upon the Earth to warn, protect, and fight if ever the Blackness should return.

And He Breathed into Man the Breath of Life, and Man became a living soul.

II

* * * * *

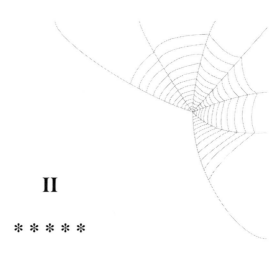

The tiny points of living fire moved back and forth as their dance with the winds progressed. Their glowing wings moved the air away from the master so fast and, yet, so smoothly, that to the untrained eye they gave the appearance of chips of fire that had escaped from their fire source and were being carried by the breezes. Their accompanying bodies within the luminosities were carried around the sleeping flowers, some higher into the gnarled vines whose blossoms also slept. Some found hollow logs complete with numbers of holes equaled only by the points of light shining in the night sky above, and the lighting of the fliers that shone through them appeared as though they were in competition. It was their world in which to play. A few even glided closer to the ground where their shadows bobbed in and out with the light from the Moon overhead. It was a dance they had attended as far back as any of them could remember. It was their portion of beauty to add to the world for the Maker. They took no note that it happened only when most of that world was asleep and, thus, missing their performance. They performed for their Maker.

Without giving heed to the presence below them, their dance carried them easily over any obstacle that came in front of them. So their wings seemed to move of themselves to lift them all the while in time with the dance above the bulk that appeared ahead of them. But as they flew on, one eye on that bulk opened, for it did not sleep, and it was very protective of its nesting area.

"Have you ever seen anything so incredible?" said Jor in a strained voice, trying to whisper while not letting his excitement take control of his voice—somewhat unsuccessfully.

Thal's face, though unseen, responded in the dark and he whispered, "And if you say it any louder, our entire village will hear you."

Jor felt his muscles tighten as if this had been in a normal time during the day and he would have responded against Thal's playful insult. But his enjoying of the fire fliers was seriously out-weighing most of his other Lessons as well, or he would not have been there in the first place. Instead, he took internal comfort in knowing that it was his own discovery that had lead them to the dancing grounds of the fliers.

"But...they <u>are</u> amazing," breathed Born, taking in the sight of the apparent living fliers of fire while still trying to get over the discomfort of disobeying his own Father's instructions. "How far will they go?" He was watching them—his gaze held fast— as they moved gracefully around the object, not darting like he had expected. It truly was as if they were dancing.

"No one knows, but—," Thal answered quickly before Jor could respond, and then turned and found himself pulling a clump of vines out of his mouth that had smacked him in the face as he walked, paying more attention to the fliers of fire than to what was directly in front of him. The other two adventurers had to cover their mouths to quiet their laughter. "—I know I have seen them all the way to the small lake," he finished somewhat more quietly, picking small pieces of vine from his teeth.

Jor's eyes looked briefly at Born and he made a noise that was unpleasant as he pushed the vines away from his face with a larger-than-needed move. "You are speaking with a mouth full of tu-lak droppings. You could not have gone all the way to the small lake and back during one evening. Your family would have known of your absence."

"They were on a Hunt with—"

Born stopped. "Wait." The others stopped, also— puzzled more at his unusual contribution, since Born was usually the quiet one. He was pointing at the group of fire fliers they had been following and squinting as though that would help him see better in the darkened wooded area. "Why did they suddenly fly so high up ahead? I do not see anything."

The other two boys suddenly became very quiet as realization began to replace entertainment. Their error was now more apparent to them than was the glowing fliers ahead of them. True, the bulk of their Lessons had been left behind not at the beginning of the entertainment of the fire fliers, but when they chose to go against their fathers' words. But why would they need them out here? What had changed? Was there danger? And if there was danger up ahead, why was Born, a member of a non-Hunter family, aware of something of which they were not? There were feelings developing in their stomachs that they were not able to store elsewhere.

"Do you see anything?" whispered Jor. He was now also squinting, a most un-Hunter-like action.

Thal was trying to control the fear he was feeling coming from his stomach by preparing to use it as he had been taught. As the Lessons were awakened, his muscles obeyed to the instructions for which they were waiting, and his arms and legs tensed no longer with fear but with the power to move suddenly upon command. With this focus away from the entertainment of the fire fliers, other sensations began to awaken. "No, but there is a smell I am starting to..." And then he felt his shoulders droop slightly as he realized that the wind shifted. That meant that it was already too late. They could now smell whatever it was that had been able to smell them. He stopped and ceased all movements except to look at the other two boys. "We need to go back—NOW." He tried to say the last word with emphasis but not so loudly as to confirm for the enemy that they were, in fact, now targets ready-made for the picking.

Thal and Jor did an immediate turn-about and with all the power that their pre-Hunter legs could summon up they plowed their way—and as quietly as Hunter-like as possible—back thru the under-growth towards their village and their home. As the bushes and low-hanging vines or small tree branches began to slap into them, they both then knew that there was no chance of them achieving a successful journey home, so they immediately began looking to the trees for one strong enough to support the weight of their sudden jump onto it and also strong enough to withstand the repeated blows that would most likely come from the soon-to-be pursuing enemy. Neither of their thoughts held a place at the moment for either of the other two boys.

Born had no idea what they were running from at the moment, but there had already been something inside him welling up, telling him that there was something not right, that he needed to prepare to defend himself. His retreat maneuver, therefore, was not the same as the others. His eyes had already located the tree necessary for his safety and possible defensive attack should it be necessary. So while his two pre-Hunter friends showed amazing speed and agility in their departure, Born's fingers and feet felt like old friends to the bark of the tree as they found his way to the needed high point for his waiting.

And it came.

The togrun didn't so much mind the dancing of the fire fliers. She was used to them. They had shared the under-growth, the fields, and even the small lake for more seasons than she could remember. But there were strangers in her area—again. Those small, strange-smelling strangers. And their walking would have them come straight towards her nesting area, and that simply was not acceptable! Her young one was due shortly, and she would not let ANYthing come near her nest, especially something new and strange, and especially not these strange ones! Everything in the area knew to give her nesting area a wide protective area, and since these strangers were not doing that, they were not welcome and clearly intended harm for her young one!

Her entire outer skin rippled—no small feat, considering its thickness. The plating along her spine clacked loudly as she did to warn off any enemy. In this case, however, it was only the result of her skin ripples which were the result of her fury at the approach of the harm-intending strangers. Her heart began pounding as it received note from the fury and the extra blood and power it sent into her limbs gave her the strength that she knew she would need to protect her coming young. The air around her seemed to decrease in pressure as she inhaled to complete the needed picture that had been carved into her bloodline for as long as she knew life. It would have been an amazing thing to see, but since it was still very dark and no one was there, the entire amazement of the event was lost as what appeared to be a moderately-sized hill became alive. In one complete fluid movement, the huge 75 ton beast jumped to her feet, the action of which caused a reverberation in to be sent throughout the earth, opened her mouth, and as the three razor-sharp horns strategically placed over her nose and head flashed their reflection in the Moon, a scream came forth from her mouth that awakened all that slept anywhere around for some distance—even as far as the small lake—to tell them that the mother togrun was on a protective run.

Born sat quietly in the tree as the vibrations reached him first from where her feet hit the ground after she awakened. His fingers closed on their own a little tighter on the hold they had. Then her war cry reached his ears. A mama togrun! His heart was suddenly beating stronger, as he could feel it thudding now in his grip in his hand on the tree. That was when he realized this tree may have been selected too soon. Since he wasn't supposed to be out there anyway, he had not brought along any weapons of protection. It was supposed to be an adventure for fun. He sighed. Once again, he realized the foolishness of not following his Father's Lessons. But the initial strength and security of the tree spoke to his fingers and his feet, and he felt he still might at least be safe from the togrun. When he got Home and his Father awakened, that would be another matter altogether. He was thankful he knew the outcome of each because of his Lessons. Still, his heart was telling him more of the togrun's charge as its beating was now faster than before as his ears told him of the increasing fury in the pounding of its footbeats ripping up the ground in its approach.

Suddenly the tree swayed slightly and a heartbeat later there was a man sitting next to him. Born barely had time to breathe, much less react. All he could do was continue to hold on to the tree and chance a look from the ground to the man as the no small discomfort set in that he had been totally unaware of his earlier presence.

The man smiled as his own hands and feet found their holds and his eyes found their focus where Born's were. "Ah. Good. You held on instead of falling. Do not be concerned about not knowing I was here. Your father has taught you well—but not that well. You have much to learn before you can join the Hunters. I have been hearing about you from Thal." He could tell Born was perplexed. "Yes, I am Thal's father. But do not be troubled about that now. We have a full-grown togrun with baby heading for our tree. Apparently we both think this one will handle her attack." His eyes had not once been on Born but had never left the place where Born had also been watching for the appearance of the togrun.

"Jor and Thal...."

"Are very far ahead looking for their own trees and...missed this one because they do not have your eye. And they seem to have left you to defend yourself—not a problem if you were a Hunter. — You are not. We may not agree with the way you teach your Lessons, but we do not believe in letting a helpless person be run over by a charging beast. And I am thinking that there is more to the Lessons your father teaches than my father led me to believe. Thal should not have left you alone and he should have seen this tree first, but he let his fear leave his stomach and get ahead of him. Clearly you have the makings of a good Hunter or you would not have been able to come tonight with them, despite your father's instructions." He shook his head, again without looking at Born. "Do not worry yourself. No father would allow his child to come into the land of the togrun during their child-bearing time. But I knew Thal would not be able to resist. That is why I was watching—to make sure no one got injured—including mama togrun, if possible. We can Hunt her later."

In the dark, it is nearly impossible to see something that is also dark. However, the reflection of the three horns in the Moon's light gave a brief reflection—more of a blur, actually, due to the speed of the charging togrun. But as the eyes of the captives in the tree tried with everything they had learned to respond to the brief obscuring impression heading for them, they failed completely. So, for all their watchfulness, Born and the man were completely unaware of when she arrived. And at that moment, their world changed as their tree was hit from below by two of the horns on the head of the charging togrun... and it snapped in half as the togrun continued its run, scooping up its head as it ran and ensuring the tree's parts were thoroughly split and separated. She lowered her head, dug a huge foot into the ground which churned up turf and rocks into the air, bringing her massive frame to a graduated and curved halt where she had a clear view of the results of her efforts. And she waited.

Born's fingers experienced extreme dismay in being unable to maintain their grasp to any part of this tree, and he found himself suddenly hurtling through the air—and aimed at another tree with very unwelcoming branches. His eyes moved swiftly and through the darkness saw in the vibrant light given off from a cluster of new fire fliers a hanging vine that stretched across his falling path. One hand reached for it while the other guided his landing-to-be as he bounced several times off the contorted trunk of this tree, sliding to a stop on the ground with part of the vine wrapped around his leg and hanging him upside down, his hair barely brushing the soft grass as he swung to a stop. The parts of things that he could see were either jumping or swinging around dizzily as his eyes searched vainly for the man, but he found their distorted view only giving him unrecognizable targets. He pulled himself up on the vine and around it, freeing his leg and, as a reward, found himself falling to the grass. The ground successfully caught him rather than allowing him to brake his fall as intended, so he found himself looking up as he stood, eyes now adjusting more quickly.

Ahead of him was part of a mountain that had come alive and was now positioning herself for a new attack after destroying the tree and bringing her prey to her. The man lay a short distance away—clearly his exit from their tree had been more demanding and definitely more injurious than Born's. The togrun pounded the ground with her forefoot, creating a mild echo in the distance, and exhaled heavily as she turned her head from the injured man to Born, and then back as if choosing. She raised her leg and brought it down again with the force of before, but pushed it behind her this time, ripping loose turf and rocks beneath it and sending them flying out behind her, and she opened her mouth and issued forth a howl that would have done things to Born's blood had he not paid attention to the Lessons of his Father.

And, at this point, the Lessons were again strong in him. Born did not stop to think. He did not stop to take in the size of the huge beast before him that prepared to protect her nesting area. As he saw the man lying on the ground and looked again at the animal, he felt his heart slowing and his breathing slowing and suddenly he saw the scene with different eyes. He *Saw* it. He did not see an enemy. He did not see a huge beast worthy of a Hunt. He saw the mother trying to protect her young unborn child. He slowly held up his open, empty hands.

The togrun suddenly stilled her shrill scream as its echo gradually faded and held her breath and then didn't move. There had always been two strangers. There were still two strangers. But one of them... was now not the same. The one stranger was standing there with its hands open. The togrun had seen other strangers like these. They all carried weapons in those hands. This one had empty hands. Maybe it was not an enemy after all. But what about the other one? She turned and focused her attention on the stranger lying on the ground.

In the absence of the attacking sounds of the togrun that had filled the air until that moment, the silence was nearly deafening. Born's own heart would have quieted itself were it not for the difference in the boy to whom it gave life. Born himself did not allow any thoughts of fear or awareness of the life-threatening unusualness happening right then. He merely stood and walked slowly over till he was standing in the path that would place him distinctly between the injured man behind him and the togrun. He turned slowly and allowed his eyes to behold the creation before him. It was a huge animal. He couldn't even see the top of its highest spire because of the angle. What a magnificent creature. There was nothing here of which to find fear. He, again, held his hands out...empty...and shook his head. "We are not your enemy. Go back to your nest," he said quietly.

She was watching what it did. It was now standing between her and the other stranger as she would be doing if her young had already been born—to protect it. A noise came from the one standing. It was not the kind of noise that came from them when they were attacking her. Maybe it was not her enemy—not right now, anyway. Maybe...maybe it was protecting the one behind it. Maybe that was one of its herd. She decided to let them live and turned to go back to her nesting area. She would remember these strangers when she again met their type. She wondered if others would act like them. None others ever had.

Born turned and knelt to the man who was shaking, but not out of fear. He said nothing but merely looked into the man' eyes. "Indeed," said the man very quietly, not yet convinced that the togrun would not return. "You have my thanks for saving my life—in—whatever way that was. It was not something a Hunter can understand. But I <u>do</u> understand that I am alive. You have things in your Lessons that no Hunter will be able to accept for a long time. I shall think on this. And in return for my not delivering you to your father, you will not pass on to anyone what has happened here tonight. Are we agreed?"

Born nodded as he helped the man to his feet. But he would be dong his own thinking on this. He would have to find a way to ask his Father about what he *Saw*. He looked up and then behind him and found his heart began racing faster again as his eyes barely made out the disappearing shape of the togrun as she disappeared into her nesting grounds. He was not aware of when the *Seeing* stopped. There were things to be learned here that were not in his Lessons, and that had never happened before.

* * * * *

III

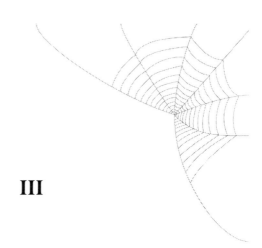

The figure remained motionless, eyes fixed, breathing barely perceptible. Had a Semsa been *Touching* , the Semsa would have smiled: even the thoughts were attuned to one sense of stillness, a total acceptance of the Truth of things. Not the truth as many understood Truth to be—as they wanted things to be, molding, reshaping them until they fit the image sought, an extension of their imperfect selves—not this self-made truth, but the Truth of things as they were Made to be: footprints, fingerprints, reflections, images of the Maker.

The Moon was being eaten by the distant ridge as the firstlight mist that had been released from the tamernan flowers slowly faded and the Sun peeked over the mountains. The orange rays cut through the shimmering green, painting multicolored shadows over the Valley as they vainly tried to catch up to the descending Moon in a never-ending race, a never-ending game—one that was enjoyed. Little ones still slept in their nests, their logs, their caves, their Homes while the Parents slept, also—or stood, ever watchful. An occasional leaf awakened, noted that it was far too early to dance since the wind, too, still slept, and returned to its rest. Silence rose to meet the lightbreak in the reverence it deserved. Movement was stilled. And for that time, all existence was together.

Narn sighed now. The Moment was over. A yawn unconsciously filled his mouth as his muscles were once again allowed to receive commands to move and carry him. It was not often that the Sun rose as quickly as the Moon set, and only during the early days of the Hot Time did it allow the tamernans' mist to be so beautiful. But it came so early!

He stretched again, his muscles rebelling, yet welcoming the movement. A smile crossed his lips as he tasted the memory that also was now stirred from its slumber. It was worthwhile.

* * * * *

He stretched. "Mamma, why is it green?"

His Mother sighed as her eyes turned briefly from the special beauty Given before her to the extra special beauty Given beside her and her hand came to rest gently upon his head. "Narn, it is best to wait until it has faded to absorb in all you can."

His eyes fell. "I am sorry, Mamma." But the beatings of the heart of such a young one are not counted the same as when he becomes older, so before the darters could scramble from one rock to another he looked up. "—But why is it green?"

She could not suppress a smile. He brought that out in her. It was a good ability of his, and she welcomed it. It helped her to be more aware of those special abilities the Maker had Placed within her. "Because that is the special affection that the Maker Gives the tamernans during that portion of their lives. It is their thanks to Him for their beauty. They use it to honor Him. They always give a mist to the Valley, and the Valley grows with life that reflects the Love of the Maker. Sometimes they even sing. That is how it keeps its beauty all year 'round. But just as you feel differently at different times of your life, so do they."

Narn wrinkled his small nose and peered out over the Valley at the unending flora. An unending stream of questions filled his youthful mind. He would know more about this. "How do they feel?"

The Mother put her arm around the small boy and gently pulled him away from the nearing edge of the cliff to walk with her. The Moment was over. It was time to return to the Home. Her eyes looked up slightly as her breath came out quietly and joined the passing breeze giving honor to the Maker. She squeezed him and guided him along back toward the path. "Proud, my son. Proud."

"Do they ever give a different color?"

The smile faded briefly from her lips—a stark contrast, one that clearly was not the way in which her face usually appeared. For the briefest portion of time, it almost seemed that the face rebelled at the loss of the expression, as though the taste of her forming words was less than pleasant. "It is said—that when the Name of one of the Great Ones is Called, the color becomes...topin."

"Topin?" His hand squeezed more tightly on the fingers it was holding as he tried to listen to the answer given him, form the next question, and keep from stumbling all at the same time. It proved a worthy feat; however, he was successful.

"It is the color of a Great One, for Its spirit rises from Its shell to return into the hands of the Maker, and the tamernans conceal It as It does."

"Have you ever seen them sing—topin?"

She shook her head. "None of us have. But it is said...that long before us..." She became silent and her eyes closed slightly as the pictures came easily to her. They were good, of good things, had a good taste. Even though they sang of something that was normally not thought of as...

"The song at the Fireside?" he asked unhesitatingly, not realizing that he had been disrespectful to her in allowing the excitement of his words to cause hers to pause.

She nodded in silence now, her eyes glancing down briefly at the top of the head that bobbed up and down next to her, brief wonderment coursing through her of how precious he was, how she hoped she was giving him all his Lessons properly to honor the Maker.

"But—it is a pretty song." The boy's eyes now turned upward toward his Mother's.

"Yes," she said, now without looking down to spill the water in her eyes as more memories filled her. "Yes, it is."

* * * * *

He turned, finding himself humming the song from his childhood as it echoed faintly in his memories.

"I wish Yad could feel this," he thought to himself, and then reflected. He was beginning to catch himself doing that more often now. It seemed that there were several ways something might be seen, depending on who was looking at it and with what set of eyes he used. Narn knew that any one individual may have several sets of eyes. But if their owner listened properly to the Lessons taught him, all sight would eventually lead the seers back to that which the Maker had Intended. There was nothing wrong with seeing things with different eyes as long as it did not take you from that which the Maker Intended. But his friend did not seem to understand this. Narn had tried to explain it to him. He had not listened, of course. His Lessons were different from those Narn heard from his Parents. In listening to the words of his friend, Narn found he often was better able to see wherein his friend had found a different path upon which to walk, one that would take his friend from that of the Maker if he were not careful. Narn listened to the words of his friend because he was his friend. He was, however, always careful to listen to those of his own Lessons at the same time. It did not always change the outcome of his thoughts nor his feelings, but it often made them more clear to him. He just wished his friend could hear his own Lessons the way he listened to his. *"But he is my friend, regardless of his feelings, "* he argued with himself. *"Of course I care about him."*

He stopped abruptly, the trees and bushes moving past him rapidly, dizzily, as he found himself whirling around, his hand already on the knife at his side. Without needing to search, his eyes moved on their own and fell on one of the larger fruit trees with a peculiar twist in its trunk. "Come out." His voice became purposefully lower, trying to equal that of the authoritative boom of his Father's. Indeed, there had been few that could ever resist it. "Come out and be seen. My knife is sheathed."

"Oh, it always is, so do not go getting big at me," came the sullen return. "You knew I was here all along." The owner of the voice stepped out, and suddenly it seemed as though the very colors of the flowers around them became more rich, more full, more...real.

He smiled now, his hand leaving the knife without being told. "Lua, I have told you about sneaking up on me."

His eyes followed closely as her slim frame slipped between the other trees and bushes and she was beside him, her long dark hair catching up with her and slightly enveloping her. A separate song was being sung by the way she moved, giving tribute to the marvelous ability of the Maker to Place so much beauty in one person at one time. It often seemed that He had Taken extra effort to...

She was pursing her lips at him. "You always know when I am there, even when you do not see me, so do not act your silly knife game with me." Her eyes closed slightly as she looked at him. They spoke silently. There was much being said.

He felt his eyes close, a large breath fill him, then he opened his eyes again. The scene before him was the same. That is, there were no changes one could see. Her eyes were still speaking to him. He noted the feelings this gave him as his eyes took in her song, then sang a different one for him to respond to. There was a different need now—his heart beat as slowly as before, allowing him the peaceful control he needed over his limbs, but the strength of the beatings had begun to increase. "You have the grace of a crippled tu-lak, Lua. It is not hard to notice you—" he looked at her again, trying to prevent his look from becoming a gaze; he almost succeeded "—in any fashion." An unbridled sigh passed through his lips.

She skillfully ignored his good words for her, as she also noted the need for a different song within her—her heart, though she was unaware, was echoing the beatings it was feeling coming from Narn, and her sandaled foot purposefully collided with his knee. "I know better, so if you do not want my tu-lak foot to do damage equal to its size..."

"I yield," he grimaced, acknowledging a partial-truth. There were some contests whose value was solely in their being, rather than in their winning. "Why are you out so early?"

"I heard you talking to Yad about coming here this morning."

He sighed again, unsuccessfully trying to hide the feeling that rose unbeckoned at the mention of his friend's name. He had learned that it was of little use to try to hide his feelings from her. She always seemed to know what he was feeling, even when he was trying to hide it from himself. He actually rather enjoyed that, that he did not have to hide things with her. But some things happened inside him no matter what he tried to hide—or not hide. He also decided to ignore how it was that she had happened to hear him talking with Yad. "Yes. He would not come."

"He said he would not?" Her eyes turned and saw the last of the mist reflecting the Moon's glow, soon to yield itself to the Sun's warmth which would send it away and dry the now thirst-quenched ground.

He kicked at the grass in one spot. "He has always said he would not; and yet, I know he must come sometimes. A Hunter must know all pictures drawn by the things around him or he may not survive someday in a Hunt."

"But why would he say..." She stopped and her eyes filled themselves with him again. His eyes were far away for the moment. "Oh. You have more meaning in your words than only what you are saying."

He smiled. She knew him well. "Sometimes it is easier not to say things that bring on some feelings. Yad would not join me in seeing it as I do. Yet, he will be here watching, too. And, although we both know that I know this, we cannot speak of it. He would never admit that he could not watch it with me. And I would not talk of it with him. It would be too painful for him, a pain which a Hunter must not allow. A Hunter must be able to see all things. In his not watching with me, not seeing with me, he feels better about his way of seeing things. My way is an enemy to his way. And although a Hunter should learn all about his enemies, he cannot bring himself to see things with the eyes of which I would teach him. And even though his own words betray him—he is my friend. So I carry this burden for him. It is often easier to hide things from yourself than from your friend."

She looked into his eyes as they returned to where they were. It was hard to know what was being hidden inside him when he looked this way. A part of her wanted to reach out and touch that part of him that was always withheld from her. But she knew that that time would come with their Joining, so she settled for words. "You care about him greatly, even though his words are not like those of your Father."

His eyes filled themselves with her now. Sometimes her ability to say the unsaid made him wonder at her—why did she not do that always? Then, again, he reflected, perhaps she did and he was the one whose ears were without hearing. He considered that, briefly, and decided perhaps he would make his ears hear her words better—for the sound of her voice to his ears was like the pouring of cool water from the river over a body that has worked long under the hot Sun. "Yes. Yad has taught me a lot. As I listen to his different words, I am better able to see the Truth in my Father's words.

"It is interesting." His hand was scratching the back of his neck as his eyes took on the far away look again. "Some of Yad's words are so much like my own, yet he means something so very different. And still, his strongest desire is to be a better Hunter—a worthy desire." Then, abruptly, as though pulled against themselves, his eyes found themselves focused again on the figure of loveliness standing before him, an act that they thoroughly enjoyed, and they told him so. The enjoyment went to its proper place and joined the other moments of enjoyment of the same sight. There were many.

Although she felt his eyes and relished the sensation, she forced herself to look back to the painting fading in the Valley. Her Lessons were in her, and she knew better than to ask him about such things at this point before their Joining. "It must be a beautiful thing to watch when the Sun and Moon sing together."

Something inside said that it was time to sing a new song within him, to feel a different feeling. Now was not the time for some things to be looked upon, nor talked about, before their Joining. The change of ideas filled him in the time it took the wings of the smallest flier to beat once, and he gratefully received them. He knew the result would draw a particular response from her, and it gave him a good feeling, the results of which he found he could not resist. "If it is such a great thing, why did you not come then?"

The song was already within her, not a new one at all—one that she frequently allowed to be sung because it allowed her to more easily follow her Lessons, and she also could not resist it. "And be here with you?"

His sandaled foot made its way to her backside, and, as she squawked, he laughed. "Peace?"

"Peace." She sighed, somewhat wistfully as she gazed again into the beauty of the Valley, longing for the time when... A quietness came over her again. He was right. Her Lessons were right. Some things were...

"I know," he said softly, watching her. "But I must be able to make provisions for my Mother first."

"I know." Her small, soft hand searched, unseeing, and was rewarded as it found its way into his, reveling in the way his enclosed it, drinking in the security it felt, longing for it to last.

His hand felt hers drink in all his gave, the warmth, the security, the strength, the love. And it returned it. There was much that could be said without words. It was a special thing that they had, to be able to speak without words, and he had learned to treasure it almost as much as he treasured her. "The time will come when the tamernans will sing their color for us together."

"I will wait."

"I know." He nodded. It was good to know.

Their hands grew tighter on one other's.

IV

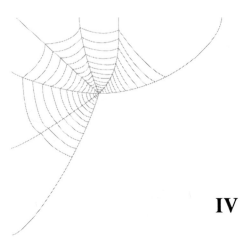

The fingers opened and closed resolutely on the bow's staff. The bow was held upright, slightly supporting the Hunter as he looked over the Valley. The fingers were prepared to grip it at any time and make it available to the Hunter should he have the need. They were ready to use all the skill the Hunter had given them to bring down whatever enemy might attack him. Or merely to bring down whatever target the Hunter might choose. The fingers did not know that the flora was too far below in the Valley for the Hunter to attain. They did not know that the Hunter, nevertheless, continued to think about being in the Valley for a Hunt. They did not know of the burn in his heart at each thought of what he might be able to Hunt should he venture even farther. The fingers only did as they always had. They held the weapon for the Hunter in such a way as to allow him to decide on the next move.

The eyes of the Hunter moved slowly, purposefully, searchingly from the edge of the forest to the far rim. The tamernans' mist had all but faded now, and it was easier to see. The individual edges of each flower were now visible, as were the limbs of the trees. In each plant might live a target, or an enemy. The Hunter's eyes took in each one carefully and let the Hunter decide if any of them were worth looking into. The eyes did not know that the flora was too far below in the Valley for the Hunter to attain. They did not know that the Hunter, nevertheless, continued to think about being in the Valley for a Hunt. They did not know of the burn in his heart at each thought of what he might be able to Hunt should he venture even farther. The eyes only did as they always had. They showed the Hunter what he was looking at in such a way as to allow him to decide on the next move. As the eyes panned to the left, a minute sparkle of light from the point of his arrow caught them, and his mind wandered.

* * * * *

The sun's light reflecting on the arrow's point hit his face briefly and, at the same moment, he felt his father's hand firmly swat his backside. He stifled his outcry, knowing full well he had deserved it. This in no way diminished the impact of the feelings of shame that surged through him, nor lessened the sensation of water that briefly tried to fill his eyes. He had been taught what to do with the feeling. The Lesson was fairly fresh. He tried to store it deep inside him so the life from it could later be used to benefit him on a Hunt. However, he found that much of it was yet only words and the feeling of shame remained. He did not like it. He determined to learn the Lessons better. He was not going to let things such as this feeling change the outcome of the Hunt. His eyes remained straight ahead, firmly demanding to be allowed to remain unyielding to the weakness. They were successful. Indeed, they had had the need of such focusing before.

"You are fortunate, Yad, that the light reflecting from your point came this way or your prey—and our evening meal—would have been lost."

"Yes, father." In one swift motion, the small, but skilled, hands moved and the sudden bent staff released its missile which hissed menacingly as it approached its target—which moved. And, just as quickly, another arrow was hurtling at it, finding its place deep in the neck as the first one passed the unwary target—which had fallen to the ground, already lifeless. The bow remained poised for another shot should one be necessary, not because it doubted the skill of the boy, nor because the boy, himself, doubted his own skill. There was no doubting his skill. That was not something that was permitted. He knew he could make any shot needed—even if it took more than the normally-required one arrow. If he could not, he would not have been asked to join the Hunt. Therefore, the bow responded accordingly and awaited his next command.

The man stood, laid his hand lightly on the boy's head, and ruffled the thick dark hair. "Well, done, Yad. You shall eat well tonight—indeed, we all shall. That flier was a full one, one of the largest I have seen."

As the boy received his father's approval, some of the shame was able to be hidden. "Thank you, father."

The father suppressed a smile. There was more of the Lesson to be learned. Pride could—and would—come at a later time. "Do not allow your success to hide your failure. You have lost an arrow."

But the boy was already off. "I will find it, father."

The fading voice fell on the man's ears as he now smiled widely. The boy's image was already small from the distance he had run. It seemed that he ran upon the very wind itself. "Yes, you will, son," he said, aware that the boy was now too far to be heard. He unsheathed his knife and started walking towards the fallen prey, but as he neared the lifeless flier lying in the tall grass, another thought filled him and he allowed himself a change of mind. It was the boy's shoot. The boy should now be able to use his own knife to prepare the flier to be carried on the walk back to their Home—even if it took longer. The growlings of the Hunter's stomach were a small price to pay for the man who would be able to watch his son take the next step toward achieving the name of Hunter.

The youth ran into the brush, the initial stinging of the branches and leaves all but ignored. The pain was a small thing to disregard compared with the value of that for which he was searching. The arrows were new and their points had been carefully made using new spearstone his father had dug from the bank of the stream near their Village. The shafts themselves had been carefully cut, trimmed, and balanced from a small, well-hidden group of Trees of the Hard Wood of which only they in their Village knew. The guides on the rear of the shafts had been especially plucked and cut to size from only the fastest fliers they had been able to bring down with their arrows. They were the best he and his father had ever put together. Each one carried the pride of the youth. He would give this pride to his son as his father had given to him when they went together on a Hunt using the added special arrows they had made together. It was something each Hunter family did. It was something in which each Hunter family took pride. It ensured that the Hunter's family remembered the purpose of the families that came before it and those to follow. It ensured that the memories of the families before it would be then shared with the families to follow it. It also ensured that there would always be Hunters, and arrows, in the family.

His eye was good. It had seen arrows miss their target before—although not too often. A Hunter did not release an arrow that might miss its target. What would be the point in that? No, a Hunter only released his arrow when he knew there would be no miss. And the Hunter was trained to know this. He was trained to know this even before he was able to carry a bow—or any weapon, for that matter. A Hunter was trained to see, to hear, to feel, to know. It was what would keep him alive when he faced the enemy. It was what would keep his family supplied with food. It was what would keep the Hunter being a Hunter. And so, he knew where the missing arrow had gone, even though it could not be seen. Its path had taken it straight past the lifeless sork now lying some distance behind him. He had taken careful note of its misdirected course as he strung the second arrow on the bow.

Or so he thought.

When he arrived at the place where the arrow should have been, he was panting more than he would have liked to admit. And now his forehead furrowed, for the arrow was not there. He ignored the gnawing in his stomach, whether it be hunger or concern for the missing arrow. Neither would bring him closer to finding the arrow.

At first his eyes searched purposefully as they had been trained. It was their sole purpose to locate any object so chosen by the Hunter. They did not want to let him down. He was depending upon them. But, when no reward came for their efforts, they began to move more widely as something akin to panic now began to come from its hiding place in his stomach's growlings and find its place within the youthful Hunter. The arrow had to be here! He had seen it fly! He could not go back without it! What would his father say if...

He shook his head. No. That was not allowed. He had always—almost—found the missing arrows. Therefore, he would find this one. He would not have to again hear the harsh words from his father describing his failure in detail. Although, he had to acknowledge that, in past searches sometimes, the length of the shadows cast by the trees were very long when he returned.

A burst of air came through his nostrils. Not this time! He would not allow it to be so! He had carefully sent the second arrow after the first, watching it as... Something happened then. Pictures came into his mind and it was suddenly as though he were still standing back there with his father. His mind saw the scene again. But this time, as he looked at the pictures with different eyes, he saw things that he had not seen before. The sork had been in the tree sitting on the branch when he released the first arrow at its neck—which had moved. The second arrow had been aimed at an ever-so-slightly different angle to allow for that movement and had passed the first arrow. That meant that...

As he saw the pictures and heard the thoughts again, the fear left him. No, it did not leave him. The Lessons had come to him as they were supposed to, and he had taken control of the fear and used it purposefully as he had been taught. He had used it to guide his thoughts so they would cause him to do what was needed. He now knew where the arrow had gone. It was simple. He almost grinned in spite of himself for not realizing it in the first place. It was, he saw, too simple.

The arrow was patiently waiting for him, stuck in the limb of a near-by tree. It had little choice in the matter. It had always had little choice. But that was unimportant. It always obeyed the laws Made for it and did as it was supposed to: after its shooting and following the indicated path, it would wait for the familiar grasp of the Hunter when he came for it. It did not take on embarrassment for the fact that it had missed. It had been carefully honed to precision. It would always find its target if properly aimed. This miss, therefore, came from the hand of the Hunter. The arrow neither accused, nor questioned, the results. Its purpose was to be used by the Hunter for his purposes. And if he chose to miss, then that was fine, too. The arrow waited.

And waited.

And the grasp came.

When Yad returned, the sork was hanging from a tree. He started to hold up the arrow to show his father he had regained it, then thought better of it and put it into his holder. There was no reward needed for the regaining of that which should not have been lost in the first place.

The father noted the action—and the non-action. Approval filled him. Yad was a quick learner. He would soon become the best Hunter in the Village. But, again—pride could come later. A Hunter does not do things for the purpose of obtaining pride. Pride may come of its own, but it is not to be sought. The Hunter does things because he must be the best to stay alive. One does not take pride in staying alive. Life is reward enough in itself. However, the father did enjoy seeing his son grow in this fashion and would later speak to him of his growth. "This is your largest prey, Yad. It is good."

The boy smiled.

Allowable. It was acceptable to take delight in your accomplishments if such a feeling did not distract you and make you the meal of some enemy, so the man added, "Soon we will Hunt the togrun. It will take several arrows to quiet him."

The boy's eyes widened of their own accord and his heart began to beat as though he were running again. The togrun!! He had heard many stories about them as the Hunter families sat around the fires! He even thought he had heard the ground tell of families of them in the land near theirs as their great numbers ran through it. He remembered how his legs had actually spoken to him of their coming before his ears added their awareness. Indeed, they were huge creatures! A great Hunt would happen with them! "When, father?"

The man's eyebrows raised. He had not expected his son to delight in such a Hunt so soon. Perhaps he was learning more quickly than the father had been aware. The father did not genuinely enjoy the feeling that came to him as a result of that thought. After all—he was a Hunter. And to have misjudged in one instance would present a possibility of misjudgment in another. This could cost him his life—or, at least a meal. He recognized the feeling for the strength of the effect it had on him and carefully placed it where it needed to be. Its life could be asked for again if he had need of it. Then it would serve him rather than weaken him as it now tried to do. Instead, he decided to let his thoughts dwell on the result of his discovery. Indeed, it would be a Good Hunt to have such a skilled one with him. There would be much accomplished with such a Hunter. And for this, now he needed to restrain his own pride. Its life went into him where it could be asked for later when needed. "Did I not say? Do you know when the cold winds will come?"

"Soon." The boy sighed. He was not satisfied with the answer, but he knew better than to ask further. If the answer a Hunter receives is not sufficient, then the question may have not have been understood, either. The boy knew that he understood his own question. Therefore, he knew that the answer must suffice until he was able to perceive its results. The Lessons were strong in him.

"So you have your answer. Know now, though. Although the Hunt will be yours, the togrun will be looking for you; but you must be ahead of him. His eyes are keen, as are his ears and his sense of smell. The wind will reveal you to him—or him to you. If he is moving, the ground will reveal him to you in any case. But as you approach him, he will be able to hear you breathe even if he can not smell you. He will turn and attack you. He will signal and his entire family will follow him. You can not outrun them. You will not be able to hide from them. Once they have started running toward you, there will only be one way to avoid being trampled by the togrun's family. You will have to be ready to receive his life first—and that of his family, if the need is there. One Hunter may not be enough, depending on his age. But two will always be enough if they have listened well enough to their Lessons—and have enough arrows. The togrun is our most fierce fighter."

The boy squinted his eyes slightly as he looked at the hungry fire which was growing hungrier in the circle of rocks. It seemed to know that there was more food for it nearby, just outside the ring of rocks placed around it, and it was constantly lapping over their edge at the small piles of gathered wood. Once it was able to briefly taste of it as a tendril managed to ride the wind and land across one of the stacks of wood. It lingered there only a moment, as it was quickly smothered and the wood moved farther away from the effects of the wind. The fire, satisfied that it must remain in its prison, acted as it was Intended and then gave heat and light to its captors.

A moment of self-question came to the boy as he briefly wondered if he were squinting because of the firelight or because he was about to question his father about something that he had not yet been told. All questions needed to be asked when they were recognized, but the timing of the asking was important. One did not ask a question merely out of a desire to satisfy curiosity. Mere curiosity could get you into trouble on a Hunt. On a Hunt, there were to be few questions. That was why the Hunter was able to remain alive. But this was no longer a Hunt, and the question nagged him; so in the end he had to ask it, regardless of the way his body acted. "Father, I heard... I heard from some of my friends—of something they called a great one, something that lives—or lived—in the Valley. They said—" He stopped when he saw the anxious look pass his father's face. It was brief, to be sure, but it had been there, and the boy knew that it was the right time.

"Yes." The father sighed. A good time for his own Hunter instincts and Mask to be used, even in the telling of stories—sometimes especially in their telling. Feelings that were brought about by memories come to life from story-telling could sometimes change the way in which a story was told, and the results might be misleading. If information was needed, then a Hunter's life might depend on this. He had known this himself once when he was young. He had determined at that time to never allow his feelings to affect the outcome of the story when his own son asked the questions. So his Mask appeared and his answers were full of only the truth—as he had perceived it to be. "Lived? No, lives—**lives**, my son. My father told me of it, too. From a time past. Words... Legends...of a great beast. Like our pack-animals, but larger—much larger. So large that you would stand in its shadow for some time before the Sun came upon you again. Its split hooves are as big as your head, harder than the Mosun's spearstone, and they will pound their victim into the earth. Between its fiery eyes, a great cone protrudes which the great one mercilessly runs through its victims. It stalks them and savagely attacks without warning, before the victim can even know it is there. Its cunning is unmatchable. It is a beast worthy of a true Hunt, marked by a true Hunter. No Hunters have sought this beast for as long as we can remember. It is said that few ever returned who sought to Hunt such a creature. And then, none returned who saw it. A more fierce creature has never lived." He looked at his boy, saw the unspoken question in his eyes. "No, not even our togrun, nor the long-toothed c'wee of D'nell."

The boy's eyes narrowed slightly, but their glow was evident. He did not mind showing his desire for this. He was in control of it.

"Yes, Yad. You would do well to Hunt and bring back the trophy of such a one. But such a thing has not been heard of, nor has anyone ventured into the Valley in our time." The man looked into the distance, repressed melancholia now mixing with desire, desire that was resurfacing and hidden behind his own Hunter's Mask. Worthwhile feelings, to be sure, but none that could be put into workable Hunter goals at this point. As a youth, he had had similar yearnings—that had not come to pass. And so he had placed those feelings with the others upon whose emotions he would draw for strength should it be necessary. If it were to be, it would come about, and the Hunt would happen. If not, then he did not need to waste his time thinking about things that were not. There were other Hunts to go on in his own land first. He was in control. He would live on. He ruffled the boy's hair. "Someday. I think that now you will have to be satisfied with the togrun—and then maybe the c'wee of D'nell when you can go from our land."

"Yes, father." The boy's own Mask reasserted itself as his eyes also held repression—of eager anticipation—as his father handed him his own knife to prepare the sork.

* * * * *

The sun's light was reflecting on the point of his arrow. Yad smiled behind his Mask, noticing his hand had unconsciously moved momentarily to his backside at the remembrance. *"Someday,"* he thought resolutely as he slowly stood, his eyes scanning the last of the green mist far below him. The mist was unaware of his resolutions. It merely did as it was Told: fade as the light of the Sun became dominant over the Valley.

Briefly the all-too-familiar thought came to him that Narn must surely also be watching the Moment. A fleeting feeling, desire raised its head and told him that he could share the Moment with his friend. As his eyes closed and opened once, his heart beat silently at the thought. He enjoyed being with, talking with his friend. The Moment would be experienced differently by them. This, then, could be... No. Recognition appeared for what it was: a simple desire based on feelings for something that was not profitable. It would not make him be a better Hunter. It would not better enable him to stay alive on a Hunt. It would, however, make his ear and heart softer to Narn's words. His Lessons told him that this was unacceptable to the Hunter, for words stored within the heart can change the way a man thinks. And the way a man thinks can determine what that man becomes. Therefore, it was not a worthwhile need and would not be pursued. He would not share the learning of the picture that was being painted. He would learn it in his solitude. It would be enough.

Thus he strove to convince himself behind his own Hunter's Mask.

The thought returned. *"Someday,"*

V

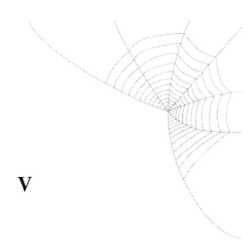

The breathing was shallow and soft. In the failing light, the tiny movement of the chest was barely perceptible. He turned to go.

"Narn?" The voice was soft. It grew softer with each passing of the Sun, but it had never taken on the coarse, crisping qualities of many of the other aging women.

He turned and knelt by the bed, the sheath of his knife dangling toward the floor. "I thought you were asleep."

The teeth showed slightly as the Sun moved and the rising shadow of the window frame covered her, and she shook her head. "No." The smile grew broader and moved into her voice. "You knew. You always do. But you are kind to an old woman." She held up her hand at the opening of his mouth. "Be still. Even if my memory failed me as it should, I need only look at you. You are a fine man. You do your Father well. I am proud."

He thought of the Hunter's Mask about which Yad and his Father had told him many times. He thought of his desire to watch the tamer-nans' mist with Lua. He thought of his unsuredness of how to provide for his aging Mother. He felt the swelling in his throat.

And he thought again of the Hunter's Mask.

* * * * *

"Go ahead," he urged. "How can I show you—"

Narn's look of perplexity increased.

Yad's blank face began to move, as though muscles were fighting themselves. There was a slight twitching of a lip, a fluttering of an eye. Then the transfixed look suddenly broke and he fought to get his breath as tears rolled down his cheeks in his now out-of-control laughter. He was still holding his sides when he finally regained his composure, and he playfully jabbed the point of an arrow at Narn's foot. "Not fair! You are not supposed to make faces at me!"

Narn's own amusement was somewhat less as his eye watched the nearness of the arrow point and his foot. "Some Mask. And you wanted me to kick your leg! All I did was look concerned!"

"Alright, so I have not mastered it yet!!" His face muscles continued to move in ways that were not totally in agreement with the sound coming from him. He was apparently struggling yet, perhaps to hide from his friend the fullness of the emotion felt. Success did not appear to be anywhere close by.

Narn grinned broadly. "Is it so necessary? You are probably the best shooter we have!"

"Agreed," Yad nodded. "But non-living targets do not usually attack, and, should something happen to me when I am Hunting, I could easily attract the target's eye. If food or prize, it will flee and I lose. And if an enemy—I might still lose. Some enemies have been said to have a fierceness in their fighting that is greater than that of even us Hunters. The Mask will hide me from their eyes." The last few words came with less strength from his heart. He found he did not like that, especially when talking about it with his friend who was always so challenging. Yad knew without a doubt what he had been taught. He had mastered the learning of the Lessons well. But there seemed to be some difficulty in his fully believing it, having never seen it. He knew the Hunter makes all decisions based on things seen or on things from Lessons so that one Hunter's experiences may help others. But this experience was the hardest to place into his life. Narn was his friend, and yet the very words of his friend were proving to be an enemy of sorts. They were giving him cause to hear them more strongly than his own Lessons, and that was not acceptable.

Narn sighed. He knew the next words. He had heard them before. They did not change. That was something he admired about his disagreeable friend: his constancy. It helped him hear his own words more strongly when faced with such strong opposition. "I know. There may always be the enemy, and you must always be prepared for it."

"A Hunter must be able to defend himself at all times. He must always be able to take care of himself so he can take care of his family."

Narn nodded. A Lesson with which all would agree: the care for Families, although the Hunters of Yad's people seemed to think differently about what a Family actually was. "There is no disgrace in only Hunting for food, you know. And there is a lot to eat that does not try to hunt us in return—or run from us if we Hunt them."

Yad shook his head in mixed amusement and frustration and returned the sigh. There was a truth in Narn's words that Yad's own father had never been able to answer for him. Yad had always been told that such thinking was non-Hunter and that he was not to listen to it. Yad found himself wondering at times why this was so, since he had also been taught that the Hunter must experience all things in order to learn from them. But he also knew better than to question his father about this. Some things, he decided, merely had to be accepted because they were taught that way. A good Hunter never questions the experience of another. It may cost him his life someday, and if it were not true, the Hunter telling it would not have lived to tell it. That was the strength of the Hunter Lessons: they were all experienced. They all were real. "Narn, will you never understand? There is much more to be gained of living than mere eating and drinking."

Narn blinked at the rewording of the Lesson his own Parents had taught him, wondering for a moment why Yad did not hear it as he did. "Yes, but it can come in ways other than the taking of life. That cannot be replaced."

Yad shook his head again. "My friend, there will always be animals for us, whether we choose to eat them or not."

Narn grunted, "Not if you take the lives of all of them" and immediately felt his face become warmer as he said it, wishing he had more control over such things when he was around his Hunter friend. Perhaps this Mask...

"You see? That is what I mean. A target or enemy could see that face on the other side of the Valley. A Mask would hide that."

"But would I want to hide what is natural to me?"

Yad blinked, reasserted his Mask—somewhat unsuccessfully—and then spoke. "You are my friend, so I value your openness with me." He swallowed slightly behind the Mask as he allowed himself to tell a truth that he had not told anyone else. "And I hope that you never lose that ability to be so open. Narn, there are some natural things that it is good to hide."

In that Moment, as Narn looked at his friend, he saw that his sharing was of something that he had kept within for all his life and Narn knew of its value. One did not say words stored within one's own heart unless you trusted the person with whom you were sharing. And in that Moment, Narn's own heart reached out to Yad in a way that neither of them could understand, nor be aware of. Yet, a completeness was made between them that was likened unto that made as the light in the sky joins the darkness as it comes to show the stars, both one in the same, just revealing it differently.

"Why not just be open to everyone?" Although he knew that even he had to hide some things when he was around Lua. He did not like that, but he knew that some feelings were not allowed before their Joining. He did not like the fact that there were some things about him over which he had less control than others, things that could make him feel or act a certain way if he did not control them. He knew that it was not right to let some feelings be in control or of great strength at certain times. And yet, he wanted the question being dealt with to be the reality he wanted. And he was discovering it was a difficult reality he was choosing. He could not be all things at all times. His Lessons showed his weaknesses. He noted that it was not the actual being weak he objected to; he just did not like being shown to be weak.

* * * * *   * * * * *

The boy was looking into the tree. He knew that he was choosing to not look into his Father's eyes by pretending to be very interested in what the fliers were doing in the top of the tree. He was afraid that if he let his Father know how he felt, that his Father would be less proud of him.

"Narn. What are the fliers doing?" The Father's own gaze followed that of the boy as the man approached his son. He could tell that something was bothering the boy. He could also tell that the boy did not want him to know about it. Inwardly, the man shook his head and smiled. There had been a time when he had been afraid to show his Father something that he was feeling. It was one of the hardest things he had ever learned to do. He hoped now that he would be able to teach his son as his Father had taught him.

Narn swallowed. "They are building a nest, Father—I think."

The man put his hand to his eyes in a mock attempt to shade them from the light of the Sun. "I believe I agree with you. You have seen this before. What is it this time that makes so fascinating?"

He swallowed again. "Well—this is higher up and—the wind might blow them around and—the eggs could fall out and—" He stopped as the man reached him and the familiar hand rested on his shoulder.

It felt good there. It made all things seem in place. Suddenly, it did not matter that he felt as he did. The feeling was still there and still just as strong, but—somehow, when his Father placed his hand on his shoulder, the reaffirming strength in it let Narn know that everything was going to be as it should. And so it was that fear took its rightful place in the back of his mind, behind the Lessons where it could no longer affect him—for the time being.

The man spoke softly to the air, not looking at his son. "Sometimes we look at things when we do not want to see something else."

The words were True. Their target was as sure as an arrow released from his Father's bow. His own was less accurate. But he gratefully accepted the accuracy of his Father's. "Yes, Father."

"What is it that you are trying to look at less?"

Truth lived. Knowing it set you free—free to be the self that you were Made to be. The Lesson was strong. It was not merely that the Lesson was fairly new. It was a powerful Lesson. "I think, Father—that it is myself."

The man now looked down at the eyes which were looking up into his for reassurance. He knelt down; the boy's eyes seemed to climb the distance as they eventually were even with his own. "And what is it about yourself that you would look at less?"

"I have found that I am not—as strong as I would wish to be."

"Indeed. That can be a frightening or unpleasant thing. Tell me. How did you learn this?"

The words came faster now, as though they had been a flier cooped up inside a cave whose entrance had just been opened and it escaped.

"I was in the meadow and a picture came to my thinking that a Lesson had drawn. I saw the picture clearly. I did not live my life and do things like the picture showed. That meant I am weak."

"Well. That **is** a hard picture." His hand squeezed the boy's shoulder slightly as everything else in his gaze faded but his son. "I have a thought—that if you have bad feelings because of the pictures you see from the Lessons you learn, you may soon not want to learn any more Lessons."

The boy was silent. Sometimes the freeing of one's heart that comes with the knowledge of the Truth that is therein comes slowly.

"No one wants to carry in his heart bad feelings for himself. But there are times when it is necessary so we may improve ourselves. If we do not know when we are making a mistake, we will not know how to improve ourselves in anything we desire to do. Narn, this is an important Truth."

Narn had a feeling that this was going to be one of those times. In the past he had grown to look forward to them. But this one— he was shown to be weak. He had always been so strong in everything. And now—to be weak. Who would want a Lesson like that?

"The purpose of the Lessons is to show you how the Maker Wants you to be. If you are not able to do that, then that is something that you can let the Maker Help you work on. Just as you let me help you better your shooting arm. I give you the Lessons in shooting. The Maker Gives you the Lessons in living. It is good that you feel the way that you do. It shows that you want to live the way the Maker has Shown us."

As the Truth in his Father's words filled the boy, Peace also came to him and filled him, driving out his feelings of weakness. And as his heart beat again, the boy felt at one with his Father and was pleased to be his son and he scrunched up his nose. The edges of his lips struggled not to curve upwards. "It is good to feel bad? It is good to be weak?"

The man smiled and tilted his head slightly. "It seems that you have returned—I think that you are playing with my words now." He reached down and pinched the boy's nose lightly. "It is never good to have the bad feelings all the time. But it is good to have them if they are showing you what you must do to be better. You remember that you did not always shoot your arrows so straight. Well, then this is like that. You practiced every day. For a long time. And now, you are one of the best shooters. It is a wise man who welcomes the chance to make himself wiser still. If you practice the Lessons of the Maker as strongly, you will be one of the best people. There is a strength in the weakness if the Maker has Shown it to you."

***** *****

Narn did not like being shown to be weak. He decided, then, that it was not the weakness he minded. He just did not want others to know of it.

"To be able to be that open would also make you open to your enemies."

Narn looked deeply at his friend. "If everyone is that open, who would be the enemies?"

"Narn, my very feeling friend. The beasts of the field will always be your enemy. And there will always be enemies just because people are different and will disagree."

"You and I disagree on many things, yet I hardly consider you to be an enemy."

"Really?" Yad remembered some of the words his father had said. "My words disagree with yours, so they are an enemy to yours because you could not follow my words anymore than I could follow yours. For you to follow my words would be for you to become like me, and that you cannot do. So, in that sense, I am your enemy."

Narn's brow furrowed a moment. There was Truth in Yad's words. But it was not like the Truth when he heard it from his Father or Mother. He listened to the words again as they echoed inside him and then Narn realized it was only a partial Truth. Which meant that it was also a partial unTruth. That was the confusion, and confusion was not of the Maker. Truth is always Truth. But Truth spoken in part can become an unTruth. "You are only an enemy if I allow your words to change me, and I choose not to do that. So I choose you to not be an enemy to me."

Yad blinked behind his Mask. It was a good answer—a very good answer. But he went on anyway, only slightly undaunted. He would not lose this battle of words without a strong fight. He was a Hunter. He was also the friend of the one with whom he was disagreeing, and that gave him some allowance for not winning the battle should that be necessary. Not that he would lose it. He would never lose it to his friend. He might just not win it. There was a difference, he noted from his Lessons, between losing and not winning. "There will always be those who disagree with you," he repeated. "Some, stronger than others. They will become your enemies. You cannot be at peace with everyone."

"As far as it depends on me, I am supposed to be peace with everyone." The Lesson ran through Narn's mind from where it had been Written on his heart.

"And you do it well. Not everyone has your ability." He pointed at his friend a moment. "You would even be at peace with the animals if you could."

Narn smiled in spite of himself and shrugged.

"And yet you must eat."

"Yes."

"And there is not always fruit available."

"Nor meat. We have been Given seasons."

"Ahhh, to find the place between the ends on the supported rod where both sides stay level. Balance. Not easily, nor often, achieved. Something else always interferes."

"Perhaps. I do what must be done, not because I desire to do it, necessarily."

Yad's Mask hid the grin. "Do I hear Narn saying that he does not always feel in his heart the things that he says and does?"

Narn allowed his grin to show. "Do I hear Yad saying that he does what his heart tells him he should do, even if he is told otherwise?"

Yad's Mask quivered, then reasserted itself. "Your words shoot straight. Your target is seldom missed." It was an admission he would not say to anyone else, and one that he was striving to vary, even in this case, although he found that part of him did not like feeling the need to be able to hide it from his friend.

"Shooting is not hard when the target is so available."

The Mask was getting harder to keep in place. The target must be altered. "Narn, I have seen you shoot."

Narn sat upright abruptly.

Ah, Yes. Yad felt this a safer direction for the words to follow. "Yes, I know you practice—and I know why. You feed two mouths now, and you are trying to be able to feed three."

Narn struggled to relax, unsure exactly of why he found discomfort in the knowledge that someone else knew of his future plans. It was no great secret. But he had not outright spoken of it, especially to this person. But if this person was truly his friend, then why was he so bothered? The question did not yield an answer, something else that Narn did not like. But he had other things to think on just now.

"You could equal me, if you tried. I would be proud to have you Hunt with me, even if only," he added with a grin, "for food."

"— — —"

"Narn—lost for words?"

"I—did not think anyone—knew." The feeling of uncertainty continued through him. Yad was his friend. Surely it was proper for him to know. But were there others? Did it matter? It was a normal thing for a young man to be thinking of such preparations. So why was he discomforted? And from his friend?

"I do not think anyone else does know. You have hidden it well, despite your feelings for Lua." He held up his hand when he saw clearly the emotion flood in his friend's eyes. *Victory!* There was no chance of a Mask there. Narn had clearly been undone by the words. Part of Yad felt as though a small Hunt had been successful. Another part felt— He was unsure, but it was not pleasant. The Hunter was not able to identify the feeling, so he sent it to its proper place to be called upon later should it be needed. "She has not said anything, nor have I. And no one else is outwardly pursuing her but you. She would not have that.— But you should know that already, or you would not be pursuing her. Be comforted, my friend. Your plans are yours, and no one else's. I am your friend, and I share this with you only because we are so close. I can sense the Hunter in you. I saw it in your father when he got food for your home—even when none was available. I know he taught you things I can never hope to see, and I do not say that lightly. There is something you have that makes your abilities even greater than mine—if you would only use them."

The words were coming from the young Hunter almost faster than he could think them, leaving him little time to wonder upon their source. "Look. I know we do not agree on this, although we both always eat our prizes. I love the thrill of the Hunt, and you would use the Hunt only to survive, and then only if all other ways to gain food had been kept or removed from you. But I know you have practiced more than necessary to be able to provide more than normal. Your tracking skills must nearly equal mine by now. But it is not something you tell everybody about." He watched his friend carefully. "I doubt that you have told anyone about it. Even—" *Carefully*. "—Lua."

Narn blinked as he gulped in air. "What—"

Yad held up a hand and shook his head. "Quiet, my friend. As I said, I know she is the third mouth you strive to prepare to feed. It is not hard to see how you look at each other. I also know that as the head of your household you feel it is necessary to be able to provide for her before you approach her family for permission to bring her into your house."

Narn's mouth was open.

"You see, just because I do not agree with the words you tell me of the Lessons your father taught you does not mean I have not listened to them. They have value, even if only to better strengthen the feelings of my own beliefs." Yad found at this he had to push aside a Lesson he had had from his own father about the words of the non-Hunters. He did not consider Narn a normal non-Hunter. He knew that Narn would never tell him words deliberately to hurt him or to try to get him to give up his own Lessons. Lessons from the family were highly valued, even from those with whom you disagreed. "But, because they come from you, I hold them of great value in my heart."

"It does not change how I feel." Narn found, however, that he did not know how to feel at this point. He had never heard Yad admit these things. It had always been easier to argue with his friend when he thought there was such a vehemence behind their disagreements. But now...

"Nor me. You are my friend, and whatever your choices that differ from mine, you will always remain that."

Narn felt the familiar swelling in his throat.

"Ah! A good time for me to tell you again about the need of the Mask."

* * * * *

And Narn looked at his aging Mother and thought again of the Hunter's Mask.

* * * * *

"It is because the Mask about which Yad would teach you is not the same as the one we use if we need to Hunt."

"But why is the Mask necessary, Father, if we only Hunt for food?"

"Son, I know Yad has told you sometimes your prey may become the enemy and turn on you. That never has to happen for us. We do not need to use our strengths in Hunting for food. In our Hunt, it will come to us—but only if we are not like all other men. The Mask helps us be apart. We do not Hunt or take life for the thrill. We do so only to survive, and so we are no threat to the animals, for all will be happening according to the Design of the Maker."

Narn pulled at his ear and thought awhile before he spoke again. He knew what he wanted to ask, but sometimes he was concerned that his asking might make him appear...less...to his Father.

The man looked into his eyes and a depth there was conveyed that bridged all parts of him that seemed unreachable, made the concerns flee as if never there, and Peace settled within him.

"Do they know that?"

His Father smiled. He really enjoyed giving the Maker's Lessons to his son. His wish was that he had been as willing to hear the Lessons as was his own son. "When we wear the Mask, they do."

"But not when Yad wears it?"

"He takes life without need. The Maker did not Make the animals for that. Yes, Narn, they know."

* * * * *

And Narn thought again of the Mask. The words of his Father and those of Yad both spoke now within him. But when two voices echo in the Valley at the same time, neither can be heard clearly unless one is stronger than the other, and thus the words did battle inside him. It was a silent and brief battle, but that did not reduce the vehemence thereof. Some words were loud and brash, and others were like a still, small voice—which could still be heard even though the others were much louder. In the end, only one set of words could remain. But it would be those to which Narn had chosen to listen, those which he had chosen to have written on his own heart. The reasons for his choice hid themselves deeply within the folds of the very place upon which the resulting words would be written, for a man's inner thoughts are not often apparent to himself and they do not always listen to the Lessons he has been taught. As his heart beat again, the battle was over. And a new Lesson was now forming in Narn's heart. The writing of the words happened between the next beatings of his heart but they forever changed the way he would see these things of which he had been taught. So it came that the words found their home and Narn knew then both of the Mask of the Hunter and of the Mask as his Father had taught him. And out of this knowing a new Mask was formed. Confusion is not of the Maker, but because Narn had made the choice within himself rather than based upon his Lessons alone, the confusion that would have normally been apparent was able to hide itself in the same folds of his heart from which he had made his choice—because it knew where was its home. A man's heart may hold many truths for him, and he must choose which one he will follow. As he chooses to think in his heart, so he is. But there is a way that feels right to a man, and that way may lead to his becoming lifeless.

And Narn thought again of the Mask. And donned it. It seemed at first that it was not a part of him. For a moment, it felt like it may never be. But moments in the time of the heart and in the time of the heart's owner are vastly different. One moment may be an eternity, during which many things might be accomplished for the effect they will have upon the shorter duration of the non-eternal. So it was that during that moment, many things were accomplished for their effect upon the rest of Narn's life, and the feeling of discomfort soon left.

"Ahh, my man is grown even more," came the soft reply.

The Mask almost fell.

The chuckle was low. "Do you think you can hide it from me?

Do you think I would not know the difference when part of you is not there? Much that I am is in you. All that your Father was is in you. I knew him well.— I know myself a little less, I think." She was silent a moment. Her heart spoke to her of the words the Maker had Given to her and her husband for the Lessons to be passed on to Narn. Those Lessons painted a picture before her eyes of a young man whom the Maker had also Given to them to train up in the way he should go. The picture in her eyes over-laid itself upon the young man looking down at her and the images were very, very close. A deep sense of warmth filled her entire being, as if the Maker Himself were Telling her, *"Well done, My faithful child."* She knew she had done all she could to create the match as her Lessons had described. She reached up and lightly stroked his cheek. Any rough edges would now have to be worked out by him on his own. He was prepared. "I am proud of my son. His heart beats strong and true. And soon, I will be proud to know that the tamernans' mist rises for you and Lua."

There was a warmth that was reflected as the name came off the lips of his Mother. There was no need to think about trying to hide anything here any longer. Narn smiled now. The Mask had lost its usefulness and had disappeared on its own. He had not missed it, nor noticed when it faded.

"Good Sleep, son."

"Good Sleep, Mother."

VI

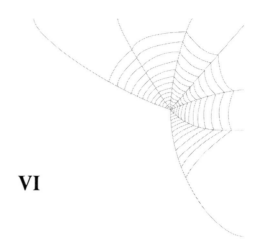

Narn stood near the fire, absorbing its warmth. His eyes scanned the off-colored trees. The wind had stopped its search for an easy path through the closely-knit leaves, and the shadows danced their cold dance less now. There was still a chill in the night air, left from the days of the Cold Time, and the fire was always welcomed—even by the youths who were responsible for building it each night. He smiled as he thought of the many excuses he had once given to avoid those duties before he realized their importance. He also thought of the words of some of the other youths when he left their companionship and chose to consider the duties seriously. Their words had hurt his heart as sure as any arrow might pierce it. But he had chosen to survive with his Lessons. He wondered, now, what those young men might be doing. Would they know how to prepare for their future households, or would they live from the Hunts of their Families, eventually having to live off someone else for the rest of their lives? Or, worse still, would they not have any Family and, having chosen a different path, have to go into the wilderness only to find the ending of their lives among strangers?

His thoughts were interrupted— "Hello, Lua" —and a warm hand slipped into his, the fingers perfectly interlocking amongst his own. When the movement was stilled, it was as if there was only one hand there again. He looked down into her dark eyes. Though their radiance contained their fill of him that they had taken in, his own eyes quickly saw her facial muscles moving ever-so-slightly.

"You always know." Although her voice carried the impossible-to-hide affection for him, there was no expression now—unusual for her, and a waste of such potential.

"A Mask covers," he noted, "and should not be used to cover beauty." A part of him wanted to ask her where she had learned to do this. He knew it was normal for someone to play at things they did not know. But the concern was about those with whom one played. Were their Lessons different from yours such that they might lead you to follow ways other than the Maker Intended? Perhaps she had seen him practicing. Perhaps...

Her lips could not suppress the smile any longer, and the natural beauty which the Maker had originally Placed there returned. Somehow, everything around her seemed to now share in that radiance. "All right, so you always say the right thing, too. You still always know when I am coming."

He shook his head and sighed. "I just listen a lot. And if there is one thing you do not need to practice, it is using the Mask."

She pursed her lips. "Afraid I will get better than you in the Hunt?"

Although there was no frown, his look became one of seriousness. "You could be the best at anything you wanted, including the Hunt.

Fortunately, you also have the quickness of mind to know which things not to try."

She looked at him directly, mouth slightly open as words failed to form on her beautiful lips. "You would—let me—*Hunt*?" The last word was almost whispered.

He smiled now. He had not realized the effect the discussion would have on her. Clearly her thoughts had been focused on this more than once...and for some time. Part of him wondered again about that as he answered. "Only with me. Hunting is for the provider of the Home, and you are not that one. But I cherish your presence in all things that I do, and anything we would do together to better make our Home could only be made better by the both of us being there."

Was it that the fire suddenly burned brighter from a sudden gust of wind or had the Moon come singing his song unannounced into the night sky? For of a certainty, the color of her skin seemed to suddenly glow, even in the dimmed light. And as suddenly, with movements that would rival any darter, she stood on her toes and put her lips lightly to his ear. And as quickly feelings of fire burned into Narn from his ear, finding its way throughout him. As his heart beat increased its speed and intensity without his issuing such a command, he thought of the Mask. Another beat and he recognized that she was not an enemy and the Mask faded. Another beat and he recognized that his own thoughts may be just as much of an enemy to him at this point but he did not need the Mask against himself. Another beat and he chose to listen to the Lesson given him by his Father rather than to the feelings of fire that even now were fighting to find their way further into him.

He recognized now the use of and need for the teasing feeling and welcomed it as it was finding its way into him and re-directing his thoughts from the earlier fires. He purposefully withheld his smile as the picture was drawn in his thoughts of what was about to happen as he softly said, "No one kisses my ear like you do."

The kiss became a bite.

He winced. "Alright, so no one else kisses my ear at all."

"I like the sound of that better." The kiss returned.

"I know," he said truthfully as the only remaining fire was burning on the logs before him. His inner fire had now subsided and been sent to the place of such fires deep within him.

"Besides," her words changed even faster than she had moved as she returned to their earlier discussion which he had avoided again, "you spoke to me before I took your hand."

He recognized her ploy and the quickness of her words. She was becoming very skillful at this. But he was not to be outdone by her. "You have been sitting and breathing too close to the boat-makers when they are pouring the bottom-sealer," he laughed.

"Oh!" Her mouth was open, but no further sound came out.

"Well. A cure for noise." He put his arm around her and squeezed, the grip surprising them both as she struggled—but only long enough for a couple of sparks to disappear as they rose from the fire, then she leaned comfortably into him. "Be still now. They are singing."

The Mosun had raised his hands and a hush fell over the people encircling the fire. His voice was soft, yet it carried the authority of the Tribe's Leader. He had long ago received the responsibility that went with that authority, nearly losing his life in the very act that won him the title. The tale was still told when he was not there to hear it, of the time when the togrun had run a path that was not normal to them. He had seen the togrun Family's path change and had been able to get to where most of the girl youths had gathered to hear Lessons about the fields. Most of those youths survived the stampede as he used every skill he had been taught—and some he had not been taught—to divert the togrun around the youths. He had also lost the use of one of his own legs in doing so. No one ever asked him where he learned to do what he had done. It was clear that the Maker had Chosen him apart from the others to take care of the Tribe. And so none dared speak against him—even the Hunters carried his respect. His voice began the song and the youths joined in.

Narn missed his Father.

"The Maker is, and He Looks on.

"The Sun speaks, his words warm us, and our lives are.

"And when the Moons speak at night, our lives still are.

"See o'er the highlands that rise from below

"Where dwell the rivers that feed by His hand

"All the lives who may come and ask.

"See in the Valley that holds

"The rivers' ends, where dwell all the lives

"Who have come and asked.

"See beyond the Valley where is the River's birth,

"Where dwell all the lives

"Who have gone and asked.

"The Semsa smiles as the Great One lives,

"And Truth lives.

"And all who seek, find;

"All who ask, receive."

And Narn missed his Father.

* * * * *

"The Maker is, and He Looks on.

"The Sun speaks, his words warm us, and our lives are."

"Father, what does the song mean?"

The man sighed and smiled inwardly. His heart was gladdened that his son's heart and mind asked questions all the time. There were, however, proper times...and improper times...for doing so. "Ask me later, Narn. It is not right to talk while they are singing." He squeezed the boy gently.

"Yes, Father," and Narn joined the singing once more. He had known the words to the song for as long as he could remember. The words were simple enough to understand. But there was another meaning held within the words that Narn had sensed for some time without knowing how or why. He felt joy enter him as he realized that tonight he would know how...and why.

Later that evening, Narn watched his Father while he was placing the firelog carefully into their fireplace so the dance of the tiny fires that went up from it would not spread into their Home, but go up the chimney as the fire directed of them. He saw that there were only a few firelogs remaining in the stack and knew that in a few moments he would be asked to go to their main storage for others, so he breathed a couple of deep breaths and spoke before his father could. "Father, tell me about the song now—about the Moons first."

The man had been moving slowly to give his son the chance to bring up the subject again before he was sent to bring more firelogs. He knew that Narn needed to ask the questions—perhaps even more than he needed to answer them. "So?"

"We only have one."

"Well." The man carefully placed the small sticks of wood around the firelog. He had longed for these words to come. He stilled his own excitement, remembering when he had asked the same words of his own Father. It meant not only that the boy was listening to what was being said, he was also listening to what was NOT being said, and it was most often through the unspoken that the Maker Gave His deepest Truths—the one that would Write on the hearer's heart the words that would later help him choose the path upon which he would walk. "So you believe we only have one Moon?"

"I have only seen one, and I have looked at the sky many times."

"Of that, I am very sure." Pictures came to him briefly of the boy gazing at the stars, seeing the pictures in his own mind that they drew. "So, because you have never seen it, do you believe the other Moon does not exist?" He continued to busy himself with arranging the sticks around the firelogs.

The boy blinked. He needed more, but he did not know how to ask his question differently, so he remained silent.

"You have never seen the stars in the day, but do you know they exist?"

"Yes."

"How so?"

"Well—" He swallowed. "I have seen them at night—and once, when the Dark Time came during the day."

"Where do they go when the Sun wakes up?"

"I—do not know. I was thinking...perhaps they are like the Moon with whom they share the sky. The Moon does not go away. It just becomes—less bright."

The man chuckled. "Good. Do not let my questions change your thinking. Keep your thoughts together.—Alright. You no longer see the large twisted tree down by the bend in the river, so do you believe in it?"

The boy's eyebrows narrowed slightly. He heard more meaning in his Father's words than the man was saying. He liked having words like these with his Father. "I saw it. I believed in it. But it is gone now. It kept our Home warm this past Cold Time. So I...believe in the heat it gave us when it went away."

"Yes. And so it is with the other Moon. We are told it once was, so we will sing of it. The songs were written about a time when it still spoke to us at night, when it sang with its brother Moon, before the Great Dark Time came. The song thanks the Maker for Giving us life in the things He has Made, and it assures us that if we follow the Lessons He has Given us, we will have a good life." A feeling of loss—one that was very great even though it was not his own—found its way from the man's heart into his thoughts, and he gently moved it aside so that it would not show in his words. This was Narn's time. "It is said the Great Ones were everywhere then, living among the people, even talking with them, each helping the other." The man rubbed his hands together before the fireplace as the flames appeared magically from within the sticks around the firelog and then fed upon it. "And the Semsa walked everywhere. There was even more than one then. People were pleased at his *Touch*. He could help them understand things that put bad feelings in their hearts just by listening to them and showing them where their walks had strayed from the path Set by the Maker." He smiled as he related the story that had been taught to him as a child. It always brought joy to his heart when he was able to share the deep things he had learned even beyond the Lessons. "Some even believed the Semsa could feel them think." The man looked over at his son and noticed the inquiring look in his eyes. "No. No one knows where the Semsa came from, or where he went. When he was here, he helped people see the Truth and accept things as they were supposed to be. When people's eyes stray from the Truth, so do their lives, and then— " He looked very solemn. "—then things become very bad. It is very easy for Man to look at things he is not supposed to see and then have bad feelings afterwards. The Semsa could understand what people felt—almost feel their thoughts like some believed. And, in sharing with them, he could help them realize where they had been captured as their paths had left that of the Truth. Once they looked back to the Truth, they could be free to live the lives the Maker had Given them.

"But some grew to believe the Semsa was more than he was, that he could do more than he could. Some even had come to feel the Semsa was something special of himself rather than that he was merely someone the Maker had Chosen to do special things for Him. And a Dark Time, the Great Dark Time, came once that was during our coldest time. The brother Moon, the one that was not covering the Sun, moved to cover it also, as though it wanted to share in the covering and shine of its own light. When that happened, that Moon broke into pieces. It is said that some of the pieces fell near here. None of them hit our land—although the people just outside D'nell think differently about their land. It is also said that the mountains were built that day that now surround the Valley. And the valley that was there became the Valley. And the other rivers that feed it were Made, too. And in the doings of all this, many Families lost some of their members. Some Families were no longer there at all." The man watched the boy's eyes closely as his Father had watched his when he had heard the tale for the first time. They were looking back at him, being filled with all that he was saying, yet there was a depth to them that could not be reached. He briefly wondered if he had had that depth when he was Narn's age. Doubting it, he continued. "And many people blamed the Semsa, that he should have known."

"*Could* he have known, Father?"

The man was silent again as the question with the different word from his own found its mark. He allowed himself a moment's muse and wondered who was enjoying the tale more. "Yes, Narn. He could have known. But to try to know about unseen things other than what the Maker Tells you can bring you bad times because you come to rely on the unseen things themselves instead of trusting the One Who Made them. The Semsa could have known. But he chose not to, preferring to rely only upon what the Maker Gave him. This is why he was the Semsa. The people did not like him as much after that. And carrying in your heart bad feelings for something—for someONE—that the Maker has Given you will lead a person away from the Maker...Who will eventually stop Giving you what you no longer appreciate."

"Did the Semsa go away?"

"No, he—well, at first he only helped where he could without anyone knowing who he was. He was doing what he needed to do with the gift he had been Given by the Maker. But it seemed that the Maker was Speaking less and less to the people. And, later... " The man's voice cracked as the realization of the depth of the loss filled him, and he cleared his throat. "And now—now, I guess the Semsa is only found in songs."

The boy looked at his Father closely. "There are those now who try to help others when they hurt inside."

His Father blinked. Who would be doing such a thing that all in the Village did not know of it? "—Perhaps. The Maker's Lessons teach us to be kind to one another. But even if the Semsa came again, he could not now let himself be known. It has been too long, and other ideas have been born by people who now feel the emptiness but do not know from where it comes."

Narn looked down. "Yad thinks differently than I do. Even some of his words are different."

The Father placed his hand lightly on his son's head and ruffled his hair. "That will always be so. But that does not make less strong nor less True your thoughts. Truth lives, always."

"Is he feeling that emptiness?"

The man's breath caught in his throat—that such questions of depth could be asked by his own son. Of a surety, he had tried to teach the Lessons in their purity to Narn. But he had never expected such words to come from him at such a young age.

Words were important. Words carried life—and the loss thereof. Narn thought about some of the things Yad had said, how he had referred to his father and the sun. How could anyone not see that they should be the Father and the Sun?! The differences were becoming more easily discernible to Narn. He had not seen them, had not heard them at first. When he used to talk with his friend and they had each spoken words whose sounds were the same, he thought they were saying the same thing. But as he listened more closely to his Lessons and they found their special places in his heart, his ear began to hear things with a different hearing. This hearing would be that which, when closely listened to, would prevent him from listening to words that would lead him from the path that the Maker had Chosen for him. "Are their eyes, their ears no longer working, Father, that they do not see and hear these things?"

"Perhaps, Narn. When you look at the Sun, and then look away, for a time you cannot see other things as well. That is not the fault of the Sun. It is Made as it is Made. The fault of the bad seeing belongs to those who choose to wrongly use their seeing. Some people have looked at other ideas and other thoughts, have listened to other words and have felt other things, and now they do not see the Truth as well."

"But—I have looked at the Sun, and eventually the bright spots go away and I can see again."

The man's breath caught in his own throat as he listened to the words again as if they were echoing from the walls of the Valley. It was only when the echo faded that he was able to speak again. Truth did not need to be defended, but the skill of listening to and the hearing of it needed much practice.

His Father's voice grew somewhat sharper; something important was about to be said, and Narn listened with all that his ears could hear.

"Not if you look too long or too often. Your eyes will indeed lose their sight. It is not the seeing of things that causes the sight to go away. The eyes were Made to see. It is what is looked upon and how long and how often the eyes look improperly. You cannot help but see things some times, but you can choose how long and whether or not you return to look at those things. So it is with seeing, with hearing, and with the feelings of the heart."

The boy's eyes looked down a moment and tried to concentrate on a small brightly-colored crawler that was looking out from under one of the firelogs beside the fireplace. It was clear that there were words in Narn's heart that were seeking a pathway to his lips. He knew that the longer he delayed in saying the words, the more different they would become from what they actually were in his heart. He also knew that his Father could usually hear that difference. But he did not like having to have the differences there at all. He wanted all his words to be Truthful before his Father. He changed positions several times, moving closer to the fire, then moving away, still looking at the crawler—or where the crawler had been. It had moved back into its place of hiding some time ago. He inhaled, tried to let the air out as though he were coughing, then inhaled slowly. "Once when the Moon was brightest, Dorn called to me to go with him and look for the fire-fliers in the field." He paused, his heart beating loudly in his ears, and slowly let his eyes climb the frame of the tall man—to rest on his eyes.

A smile was the reward, the action of which reassured the boy. The voice was softer. "I know." The Father had been waiting for this story. He was proud of his son for his trust and the way the Truth was stored in the Lessons in his heart.

Narn blinked and he swallowed. "I—I— You knew?"

"Yes."

"You did not punish me."

The man reached over and gently squeezed Narn's shoulder, knowing the lack of action itself since Narn's secret adventure had been punishment enough for the boy. He was thankful that that was the way of Narn's heart. He knew it was not so with some of the other sons who were not his own, and he quietly thanked the Maker for the Gift of his son. "Tell me what you learned."

Narn blinked. Like the waters of the stream that pressed upon its banks when it was too full, a mixture of feelings flooded into him, and he was unsure of which one to let take control. So he chose to ignore them all and speak the words as they came to him. Truth lived. "I did not go with him at first. He came to my window and told me how pretty the fire-fliers were."

"You did not go at first?" he asked, knowing the question would cause his son to reaffirm his answer.

"No."

"Why not? Did you not want to see them?"

"Oh, more than ever! I had heard about them from several of the other boys, too."

"Yes?" Some things would never change, it seemed.

"Wellll... I did not go because I knew you had told me not to go into the fields at night."

"Do you remember why?"

"It was dangerous?"

"What kind of danger?"

"I—I did not remember then. I only knew you had said, 'no'."

"But you did go?"

"He came back to my window for several nights. The more he told me, the more I wanted to go.— So..." The voice sounded, ever-so-slightly, as though it were going to quiver. Then, the boy filled his lungs full of air and let it escape. His voice was again steady. "... so—I did."

"And?"

"And he was right! They were the most beautiful thing I had ever seen. But..."

"But...you liked seeing the fire-fliers?"

"Oh, yes! They were all that he said they were. But—"

"But?"

"But, I did not like the way I felt the next day."

"You were afraid I would find out and punish you?"

The boy thought a moment. He remembered his feelings now nearly as strongly as they had been then. It had been a valuable Lesson. He had learned much about obedience. He nodded, then he shook his head and looked slightly confused. "Well—the answer is both yes and no. I mostly felt bad because I knew you had told me not to do something and I had done it. I did not like the way I felt after that when I was near you, because I felt like....like I could not be all of me anymore with you. I had to hide part of me. So, I did not go the next time he called me."

"You were fortunate in your learning."

"It was hard."

"I know." The man sighed, the knowing filling him. "Once you listen the first time, it is hard to stop listening. And eventually you will listen more to other wrong things. You could not help hearing him call you, but when you listened to what he was saying, and when you allowed him to return to your window, you listened more to his words than to mine."

"I am sorry, Father."

"I know, my son. I am proud of you. You learned well, and quickly. Some have not done so."

"Like Dorn?"

"Yes, and he will learn hard Lessons as he gets older because he is not learning the easy ones now. So it is with feelings in the heart. The more you allow in feelings that are not the ones you should feel, the easier it is for them to come back. And so, some have lost their sight to the Truth by looking too long at other ideas and feelings."

"Their Families tell them Lessons different from yours."

The boy's insights were amazing. "Yes."

"And they believe their Lessons are the right ones."

"Yes." And now would come the questions, the answers to which would help the boy choose the path upon which he would walk. The man silently asked the Maker for wisdom to give his son what he needed to hear.

"If their Lessons also tell of the Maker, how are we to know which ones to listen to?" The boy watched as something happened which was rare. He normally enjoyed watching rare things, as they were not likely to happen again when he could see them. However, this rare instance was not one of those times. Actually, as he watched, he became a little unsettled. It had come quickly, so he had been totally unprepared for it.

The smile left the man's face. Not just his lips. His entire face expressed the absence of the smile. It was not that he was frowning. The smile had simply left him. It had even left his voice when he again was able to speak. "Narn. Are you telling me that there may be Lessons of other Homes that you listen to more than those of ours?"

The boy very slowly, and cautiously, shook his head. The movement was barely perceptible. But it was an answer. For his voice had stopped in the Moment.

"Their words and mine come from the same Maker. But our hearts are different, and we may say the words differently. You have been

Given to me by the Maker to bring up in His ways. The words He has Given to me are the only ones with which you need to be concerned. You will hear the others. You may even eventually be able to talk about their differences. But for now—mine are the only ones for you. Do you understand?"

The boy nodded.

The smile returned. It had been the only time Narn had ever seen it happen, and he would remember it for always—the day the smile left his Father. It had been a solemn Lesson. It would not be forgotten.

"So, you have heard, then, other words? You cannot help hearing them, just as you could not help hearing Dorn call to you. But you do not have to listen to those words, just as you did not have to listen to Dorn's call."

The boy nodded now, gladdened that the words between them had returned to normal. It had been a horrible thing to not be able to have words shared with his Father—even for a Lesson. "Yes, there have been other words. Especially from Yad."

"He is a Hunter."

"???—So—are you?"

The man nodded. "But only when needed. Yad would hunt even if there were nothing to Hunt. So his words will be like ours, yet different."

"And some are very different. They do not even believe that the Great Ones live—or lived."

"Lived? My son, They live on. Just because They are not seen does not mean that They do not live."

"The Great Ones went to the Valley?"

"It was necessary. The Ones that did not, had Their Names Called." The man stopped and his head turned slowly to regard the boy. There was more there than had been with him when he was Narn's age. "How did you know they went into the Valley?"

The boy shrugged. "They are not here. They must be there."

The man's smile became a chuckle again. He recognized the thoughts behind the words. "So you have been asking your Mother, too?"

The boy's eyes widened, but when he saw his Father's response, he relaxed. "Yes."

"I do not mind. It is good for you to ask her questions. You will learn your Lessons from her heart in a different way than from mine, but they will be the same Lessons. As you grow older, you will hear more differences in the words of others. Hear what they say and listen to their words alongside of those of the Truth that you have learned at Home. Then you will see the Truth even more so, for if they have unTruths, they will stand out as does the darkness of the cave against the light color of the hill into which it opens."

"Father?"

"Yes, my son."

"How did you know—how did you know that I had gone to see the fire-fliers?"

The man's memory drifted a moment back to the time when he was the age of his son, when his friend had come to his window at night and beckoned him to come to the field and watch the fire-fliers, when he had disregarded the words of his Father. He had not been so fortunate. He learned first hand about the dangers of the fields at night. It was fortunate for him that his friend had been a Hunter, for it had been the skills of that Hunter-friend that had saved them both. It was that experience that had caused him to ask his own Father more about the ways of the Hunters. "Some things you will learn later and the learning will remain with you longer than if I tell you all the answers. This is one of those things." He reached over again and swatted the boy lightly on his bottom. "And right now, your Mother needs me, so off you go to sleep."

Narn did as he was told, listening to the reassuring footsteps of his Father going to his room, the man's words echoing in his thoughts.

* * * * *

And Narn missed his Father. Until his thoughts were interrupted.

"Narn?" Lua's soft voice was even softer in his ear. "Is your heart troubled? Your eyes—they look—so far away."

Some things needed not to be shared but to be stored in the heart. He sighed and squeezed her closer to him, enjoying the warmth that came from her even more than that of the fire before him. It was answer enough for then. It had been worthwhile.

VII

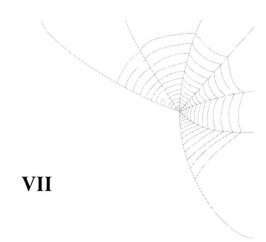

Even though the Maker had Made all places with the same importance, there were some that held special value in the hearts of Man. Narn and Lua had found one of them by the river. Lua was dangling one foot in the warm silently-moving water while Narn lay with his head in her lap. She had been learning that some times were better left to each other in sharing silence. But sometimes it was hard for her to determine when it was one of those times. Narn had been spending more time to himself, something he called his Quiet. He seemed to just sit and think. She wondered what he could think about so much—especially since it was obviously not her about which his thoughts were so occupied. She did not feel comfortable yet in asking him about such things. She knew that some things of his heart would be shared with her when he felt it was time, and that some of those would not come till after their Joining. But it made her feel—left out, apart from him...not a part of him—when he was this way, and this was not pleasing to her. The desire was great within her to be a part of everything about him, and part of her felt something her Mother had called resentment about not being able to share this with Narn.

She recalled in the Lesson that her Mother had told her that feeling came about when a person did not like the thing that was happening to him right then, that he had a right to have something else happen, something more to his own personal liking. Her Mother explained that in following such bad feelings, the person owning them would be lead down a path that would take him away from the one Intended by the Maker because He was the One Who Made their paths, not themselves. She had always pushed the bad feelings aside quickly because she had been unwilling for anything to spoil their moments together. From her heart, the words of her Mother echoed faintly in her, and the thought came to her that perhaps she had been doing the right thing, but for the wrong reason. She had been pushing the bad feelings away, but not because she needed to do that in order to remain on the path so Called by the Maker, but to allow herself a more pleasant time with the man for whom her heart now sounded its song. Briefly, she wondered if she wound up at the same place by using a different path, what would be the harm in that? The question found its place inside her and her thoughts about it made it louder than the memory of the Lesson so told by her Mother. Thus, what began as something small, the question began to burn itself a new home, words that were once only words now became something upon which sat other questions, flinging themselves at her. This picture forming in her mind would have been clear to her at another time, and the danger of it also clear because of its hiding the words of the Lesson, and, thus, their Truth. But the desire for her to be able to share more things with Narn burned more deeply within her now than it should have, and so she disregarded the other Lessons from her Parents as well.

There might have been a point during which the very nearness of Narn would have caused her to question her own feelings; but now, as she heard him humming quietly but was not able to recognize the song, the resentment was able to move in unhindered, and the questions seemed to leap out from their places of storage, demanding that she be allowed to share in this part of his life, and she yielded—trying not to look directly at him. "Narn, what are you singing?"

He opened his eyes abruptly and blinked. The humming stopped. "Why—I do not know. I was just—" He stopped, puzzled. A moment ago, all things had been together, a mixing of them into a oneness that was Foreseen by the Maker. He was feeling that oneness weave itself throughout his being, enthralled that he could be able to feel such a thing and still be lying there by the stream. But now...there was something missing, as though he had just awakened from a dream and was trying to remember...

Her feelings of him not sharing something with her were too strong for her to notice that there was now something different about him. "Sing it for me."

And because he was still so close to the middle of the world from which he had come, he did not notice the difference in the way she spoke to him. He merely responded in the way he always had—to the simplicity of her request. He closed his eyes again and let the sounds of the surroundings fill him. All of the things Made were singing their own songs, and it was beautiful. It was good to be able to be a part of them and to share in the singing of their song of oneness. One merely needed to find his Quiet and... the song of oneness came again and filled his being, and... the humming began again. Then, from a place of which he knew not, words aligned themselves with the music as it reached his lips—and formed words. He had never before heard the words, so he found himself listening—as well as singing—as they came forth.

"Sing, Fabra, sing, for tomorrow will come

"When freedom will ring where the Semsa is from.

"Fly with the sork and see with his eyes

"Of the choice at the fork and the stopping of cries.

"The mist stills your fears while the night breathes her breath.

"The Great One appears; bring She life, bring She death?"

And then came the great difference. The joining of the two worlds closed as the song ended. What once was full was now left seeming... less. What once was an answer was now a cup that brimmed with questions. For the music had stopped, the words were no more, and his lips were silent. Yet there was a feeling left within him that...

When the heart has listened more to words and feelings that are other than those of the Lessons from the Parents, the owner of that heart will also be almost without hearing of the song sung in oneness by those all around him. Or her. And so it was that the fullness, the richness, the oneness of that which Nam spoke went...unreceived.

But that did not make the Truth any less, nor its effect.

Her eyes grew wide. The misunderstood reality of what had just occurred was so strong within itself that the question burning within her had been quenched, and along with it—for now, the resentment. And, so, that which separated them was, at this point, now without strength, so it retreated back into the cave, the home of darkness it had made for itself in so short a time.

Her voice was barely a whisper. "What is that? I have never heard such a song!"

Narn sighed deeply, his eyes opening slowly. A feeling, *unTouched*, unrecognized, was disappearing within him. It was like an echo coming back from one of the steep rills in the Valley, fading—when there had been no voice to cause it. The more he tried to hear it, the softer it became. "Neither—have I." He swallowed as the impact of his own words struck him.

"What?" She looked directly at him now. It was almost as if she had never seen the person lying before her.

He blinked. "I mean—I have never—heard it sung—" He struggled to speak the Truth in words that made sense. "I have never sung it before. I—only learned it—recently." His head felt light. The echo was fainter. He yet strained to hear it.

"It is pretty," she went on, barely noticing the state of the man by her side. It was not that she was insensitive to him. It was merely not within her to be sensitive to that of which she had not yet become aware. So she also tired to speak words that made sense. "The words are not like those of the fireside song—or any other I have heard." Then, suddenly, as if she was trying to recognize who he was, she said, "But you have always been good with words." She stroked his forehead gently with her fingertips, and they spoke to her now with more words of unfamiliarity. The furrows in his brow seemed rougher than the fingers remembered. They retraced their steps, as though walking again over the same ground would change what they already knew. But it was not to be. "You must be tired," she said finally, trying to conceal in her voice the regret she was now beginning to feel in her heart at finding he could be tired even when she was around. She again found herself trying to hide the feeling her Mother had warned her about, the one she felt when she was not part of what was happening to him. It had returned—and quickly, living in the strength that her disappointment provided for it. The result left a sensation in her stomach that she did not like. She had never felt anything bad while being around him. And she had resolved that nothing must be allowed to ruin the time she was able to spend with him. She breathed deeply for a moment as she had seen him do. However, she did not notice any change in her feelings, nor in the pit in her stomach that was becoming deeper. The Lessons from her Parents did not speak to her now as they had earlier, so she had to face this on her own. And she would. She would not let anything spoil their time together, not even her own silly feelings. She wanted earnestly to feel only the closeness they always shared. She spoke with more conviction—at least, in her voice. "Yes. You are tired. Let us go back. We can talk later." She would, perhaps, talk with him later about these feelings and what they meant. He had always been able to help her better understand her feelings.

"Yes." He sat up slowly, noticing, yet not fully discerning, the changes in her voice. There was more in his mind now than her words, and although it was usually they alone that filled him when they were together, something was happening now that was nearly as strong. He puzzled briefly what that might be, but he found it difficult to think solidly about anything else right then. His breathing was a little faster than usual, his forehead still unsmoothed as the words of the distant song continued to ring through his memory, finding now a permanent home where they had never before lived. But the echo was gone.

VIII

The sork turned the edge of its left wing slightly upward and began its slow, wide descent around the scattered brush below. The wind rushed past its ear slits, singing a shrill song that grew ever-increasingly higher, the air going faster as the speed of descent increased. It was a familiar song, that of the air. It told the sork of many things. How far away was the ground beneath him. How swift were the strokes of his wings. The coming of other winds that would be less favorable in which to fly. He opened and closed his beak slightly, feeling the wind go over his tongue. It tasted of the dryness of the area. It was a new taste to him. The skies of his land had reminded him of low flights near the streams or the lakes. This air tasted of the lack of such things. His sharp eyes told him the same thing about the ground far below in the diminutive light. There was little water here. Likely there would be little water cover when firstlight came, so there would not be the normal variety of animals to pursue either as he was used to seeing in his own land. Thus he had chosen a different time of the day in which to improve his skills. It was not that his skills were so unrefined that they had not provided with ample food supplies in his own land. It was not that there had been notice among others of his feathered wing who had spoken to him of his lack of skills. No, he was not here because of the way his skills were in his own land. He was here because of his desire to use those skills in a place of which no one else had use theirs. He had not flown this far from Home before. There were plenty or v'rill to chase around back in the forests or out in the fields of Home, but he had found himself growing tired of these chases—even though he had always been successful. Indeed, when one's skills are sharpened to the point that one always succeeds in what one does, there is no improvement. And he felt the need to improve. He needed to be the best sork in all the ways he could be. There was no room for anything less.

These Truths were not conscious thoughts in the mind of the sork. But in the instincts upon which his feathered Tribe had been Made, the desires to be the best were there just as strong. The Truth was always there, whether the Dwellers —both feathered and unfeathered—were aware of it or not. And its effects were the same, whether the Dwellers were aware of it or not. That is why it was so important to be aware of one's surroundings and how they were to be viewed with the Lessons that the Parents had taught. All Parents taught Lessons. But not all Lessons were the same. They all had come from the same Source, but somewhere along the way, sometimes the stories were gradually changed until they no longer told what they were Intended to tell. The tellers were not always aware of these changes, nor were those who were being told. It was not that all these tellers had purposed in their hearts to tell the stories, the Lessons, differently. But because they were not the best they could be, because they were not perfect, because they were only an Image of their Maker, sometimes they did not repeat exactly what He Gave them to say—unlike the Moon that so perfectly reflected the Light that He Made. The differences could only be discerned by those who had heard the Lessons told to them in ways and by those whose wisdom had not allowed such changes. Their ears heard the differences, and they tried to tell of this to the others. But it was not so with the ears of the others. And so, Confusion was wrought.

Some were aware of the Confusion. Many were not. Those who were aware tried to tell the others. But when you have been born without sight, it is difficult to understand what is meant when someone talks to you about how beautiful the clouds appear or how arrayed in splendor are the colors in the sky when the Sun prepares to sleep. Those now born into imperfection were without the understanding and often believed <u>their</u> way to be Truth, despite the Lessons they were taught. So when they changed the things they had heard to be more like what they felt them to be, their Lessons became unLessons. And as these became more told, they affected many more. Thus, in a short time, many were the ears and hearts who were born without understanding concerning the Confusion.

Occasionally, for reasons unknown to the hearer or the teller, the heart of one who lives in Confusion has words written upon it that cause that heart to question the things it has been told— those things that are causing the Confusion. These words also cause it to listen when other words come to the ears of the one to whom that heart gives life. Then another Confusion comes: to which collection of Lessons and words does the hearer then listen? Which set of Truths are the ones that genuinely came from the Maker as He Intended them to be?

Some of these ones to whom Confusion has come choose to listen further, that they might become wise. Some run from the Truth. The Truth, indeed, can be frightening at times. Some fight the Truth. Some merely ignore it. But there are those others who listen some, question some, listen more, question more, then have the new words written upon the walls of their hearts along with the other words, thinking that in seeing them both, they will not stray from the path upon which the Maker would Lead them. Such is the result of Confusion in one's life.

It is a difficult task that they have chosen. Any words that are other than those of the Maker will take their owner on a Journey to Destruction. And broad is the gate and wide the path that leads to Destruction, but narrow is the gate and difficult the path that leads to Freedom, and few there be who find it.

So, sometimes it must find them.

Although these Truths lived while the sork glided and circled in its personal flying, none of them were of concern to it. It had not been Made to have concern as such. It merely did as it was Made to do, as it had been shown to do by its Parents—with a few personally-selected improvements of its own, one of which was that it was now not in its own territory.

These Truths were of concern, however, to the one on the ground who watched the sork. These Truths had been discussed long ago with his Parents. He was told that these were important words, words that taught one much about the way that things were. And, of course, they were words that held a different Truth, one that was for the hearts of those who could not live as strongly as those who Hunted. The Hunter Parents explaining this to their son knew that there were those non-Hunters whose words were not like those of their Hunter hearts, but that was not a reason for concern. The words of others were never enemies to them. They feared no one, no thing, and certainly not mere words. Fear itself was not an enemy, either. Fear was merely a thing to be captured and used to give strength. They knew that to not listen to others would prevent them from being strong in some situation. And they must be prepared for all situations. They would simply master their own Lessons in their own hearts and thus not be affected by the words of the non-Hunters. Occasionally, one of the Hunter young ones asked why the non-Hunters could not think of them the same. This one was then told that the non-Hunters simply were not as strong as the Hunters, so the words of their Lessons taught of a living that was not as strong. So the Hunters learned to live with the non-Hunters and to view most of them as non-enemies. They were, of course, unaware that their Journey was on the path that would lead to their Destruction.

The watcher on the ground tracked the sork as it flew. He had never before seen a flier of such size, of such mastery of flight. He watched for awhile in near-admiration as the flier was in total control of its world. It came to the Hunter that such a flier did have a home in his world, and he found in himself a brief question as to where the home of this sork might be. A part of him felt almost sad at the taking of the life of such a thing of grace, the ending of the existence of such a thing of beauty. But then, he heard the words again, and knew those were the words of his friend. He recognized their place and the need for them. But the words of his Lessons were also there, and they were stronger. They reminded him that there would always be other chances for other beauties, and that the chance for a meal may not again occur. He marveled for a moment on the way the words seemed to talk with each other, each producing feelings in him that caused him to listen to first one, then the other. His decision, he realized, would be made on the basis of the words to which he listened the most. There was, however, no question as to which he would listen the most. It had always been so and would always be. He was a Hunter, after that of his father. But...the words of his friend brought about feelings in him that he found— pleasurable. He knew, as a Hunter, that such feelings could turn the eye from the target long enough for the Hunter to become the hunted. But, they also did bring about...

The Hunter felt his lips involuntarily form a smile. He knew where it was leading. He had been down this path before. He could not allow himself to hear his friend's words too strongly at this point. At another time, perhaps. But now, he was on a Hunt, and there was no place for such words here, regardless of the things they made him feel. Words would not put food on his table.

As these words and realizations found their stronghold in him, his eyes gazed momentarily, lingering on the object of beauty high above him coming closer with each moment. Soon it would be close enough to be within reach of his arrow. It would, indeed, be a nice catch. His parents would be pleased at him for this. He found it pleasing for reasons beyond the pure practicality taught by his parents. For him, it also meant that there were other things elsewhere that he and his Hunter-friends could venture out and Hunt. They did not have to remain where they were, bound by the rocky walls or the area of fire far away. This idea made his heart glad, for he, too, wished to venture into areas wherein they had not before gone. He may even find others like himself who lived for the Hunt! He found himself, briefly, wondering what those others might be like that could dwell atop the cliffs of rock from which poured the water for his river, those who might live beyond—or even in—the land of fire. Other Hunters... He felt his heart quicken slightly at that thought. It distracted him momentarily, and the speed and the distance of the coming flier were misjudged. He allowed a small moment for an even smaller self-rebuke, realizing again the wisdom of the Lessons of his parents. Such a lack of command of his thoughts, especially on a Hunt, could cost him his meal—even his life, if Hunting an enemy. He joined his bow with an arrow, making it now the thing for which it had been created.

The sork kept his eye close on the area he was circling. He knew that there was likely prey there. He had seen the movement earlier. And the fact that it was no longer there made him even more sure, for it had stopped when he had begun his descent. He prepared for his morning meal. He knew his Parents would be pleased with his find. As he prepared to arch his wings for the final attack move, there was a movement below that was unexpected. He tilted his wings back so that he could circle up and review the scene. As he began to climb higher, the lessened hissing of the air past his ears allowed another sound to enter the hearing slits. He had not heard it before. It was like another air was passing over his own, coming from below him and getting closer with each breath he took. Then there was a sudden fire in his chest and he found it harder to breathe. What was wrong? His wings no longer carried him on the air as they once did! Why was there so much heat in his chest? Why did the fire burn the air from within him? What was wrong? Why did his wings carry such a heaviness? Where were the songs of the air? What was wrong? Forgetting the would-be prize he once sought below, he decided that he needed to be able to get back to his Home to ask his Parents about this. But, he realized, Home was far off—much farther than he had let himself know. The sky seemed to becoming darker, but this could not be, as it was firstlight. Why was the ground rushing up toward him instead of the clouds? Perhaps...perhaps he should have listened more to his Lessons and not ventured so far from his Home land, on his own path. Perhaps...

IX

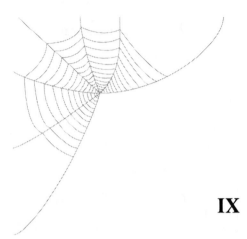

The next afternoon, Narn was sharpening some points for his arrows. His skilled fingers held the sharpening stone at just the right angle so that the new point was gradually taking on the shape he needed. With each movement of his hands, the shape before him was more closely becoming that which he had seen in his training with his Father. The history of the arrow points sharpened and used by his Father was well-known, even among the Hunters. So much so that he had been often sought out by other Hunters to learn his skills in making the points. Narn remembered that his Father had always made things simple by saying he just made them the way his Father had shown him, with no changes, and that if you kept the Lessons pure, telling them the way they had been told back to their Beginning, then whatever you created would be the closest thing to perfection, as if the Maker Himself had… "Hello, Yad," he said without looking up as he continued to work on the points, "I thought you—"

"Someday I shall also learn how to do that, and then no one will be able to Hunt better than I." He stuck the end of his bow in the sand

and gazed at his friend, silently admiring the skill in the hands that was creating such near-perfect arrow points.

"Do what? And no one can Hunt better than you now." He looked up now, blowing the fine dust from the point, and grinned.

Yad was shaking his head. The things his friend could do were sometimes truly amazing, but his eyes were now focused on the points he was fashioning. Although the points were made from the spear-stone, their finished surfaces were so fine that they now reflected Yad's face. There existed nothing that such a point would not penetrate. He finally was able to tear his eyes from the points. "To be able to know when someone is approaching."

Narn made a face. "I just listen a lot." He wiped the water from his brow that threatened to run into his eyes, dripped it onto another piece of spearstone, and started moving the sharpening stone in its slow, methodical, creative path. "I thought you were going to Yurell to Hunt sorks."

Yad drew a picture in his memory of the water from Narn's brow being used in the sharpening of the point—he would try that the next time he made his own points—as he looked briefly from one side to the other, then shook his head with a sly grin appearing on his face. "So I have said. So many think. It is my desire that they think so. But I have other desires. You are my closest and most argumentative friend, and I want...I want to tell you...about those desires which try to consume me. Your thoughts hold a special place in me."

Narn felt something happen inside him. He suddenly saw a Mask assert itself over Yad, but it was of a different nature. This troubled him, for it was the nature of the Masks that they were not supposed to be seen—a nature about which he often wondered, since he seemed to be able to see them easily. Yad was wishing to be real with him—to be truthful with him—but was not able to. There was something else there...something that was between them...something dark...

"I go alone, and I go—"

Between the next beats of his heart, Narn saw something happen in Yad. There was a lessening, somehow, of the light around Yad, as though a cloud had passed between him and the Sun, yet there were no shadows. The air around Yad became momentarily chilled. Normally, it would not—could not—have been noticed. But Narn's eye now carried the Lessons of his Father and the experience of a maturing Hunter. So he not only noticed it, it fairly leaped out at him. He did not know what it meant. It was not such a happening that one could observe again and think about after it had occurred. It merely was. But he saw, in that moment when the Sun stood still in the sky, this darkened space around Yad go into him and then come out again. As his heart beat again, the Sun shown as it always had, and all else around them was as it had been, as though nothing was different. But Yad was then different. It was not a difference he could see. It was not even one he could—feel. But there was a difference. Narn did not like the difference. Before he had been talking with his friend. This person before him was still the same person as before. But somehow, the part that was the friend had been hidden. It was not gone. It was not weakened. If anything, it seemed stronger. And, for whatever reason, that required it to be all the more deeply hidden for the moment. These things were not in Narn's conscious mind. They merely were now a part of him. All that he knew was that part of his friend was no longer there for him.

The Mask was strong now. "—to D'nell to Hunt the long-toothed c'wee." His eyes found the ground suddenly more preferable than the eyes of his friend, and his breathing became slightly faster. He inhaled deeply to control his breathing and then said in a near-normal voice, "You must not reveal where I am going until I return."

Narn dropped his tool. Or, to be viewed more through the Truth, the tool fell from his hand. His hand did not receive orders to loose its grip. It simply released it, as though it had perceived on its own that the instrument was no longer a part of what was important. In the past his hand had gone of its own accord to his knife when danger may have been present. Now it had done something else that was necessary and did not require thought or direction on his part.

Normally his senses were very clear. They were especially clear now, having spent the better part of the day focusing on the sharpening of the arrow points. He was unsure, however, of what his senses were telling him this time. It had come as a reflex. It had been done without thinking, almost unwillingly. And yet, it was something that had to be done. It was necessary. His closest friend stood before him and was doing battle within himself. The turmoil of his heart was evident. He was not able to put into words what he wanted Narn to know, what he needed him to know... Nam realized then that he must help his friend without him knowing it.

Narn's eyes looked deeply into—and beyond—Yad's. Yad's eyes filled him. Yad filled him. Feelings screamed at him. His feelings, and Yad's. Feelings he knew. Feelings he did not know. Feelings he would never know. Yad was going to... He must not let his friend... But he must...

His thoughts did not obey him like they usually did. This had never before happened. Even when his thoughts were muddled when he was around Lua he was usually able to think clearly. He found he could not even hear his own thoughts, as though they had become unimportant for the time being. Something now was more important than what he had inside, than that which was himself. He had to tell... his friend...

So why could he not speak?!

He searched frantically for the Mask that Yad had so skillfully taught him to wear, the differences of which his Father had explained. The emotion with which he began his search was a puzzlement to another part of him. He could not control what he was feeling, and that lack of control was hurting his ability to see things clearly. It was a certainty that the Mask was needed. Therefore, it would be used. It was quite simple, really. Why was such a strong feeling used to put into effect that which was needed? That strength would possibly be needed for a Hunt. Or to thwart the pain from an injury in order to survive or help others to do so. But now?

The thoughts ran through him, not as thoughts, but as things—things alive unto themselves—things which had once been and things which were now a part of him. That part was called upon and it came forth. He found that it came easily. It was not in hiding. It was where it needed to be for his use. Yad had done his instructing well, and his Father's words were also in him.

The new Mask was easily produced, although another part of him noted during the single heartbeat of the smallest of crawlers that there was now something different about it—something that made it seem as though it would now never be fully a part of him. And although it was in a small part and in the briefest instant of time, he did not question it. One does not question Truth.

The Mask came—and although his voice returned, when he spoke, it was more of a releasing of his air carrying something that had been trapped within him. "Yad!" It came out more as a word than a name.

"I know it is dangerous, but..." Yad was not looking at him anymore.

Narn was not hearing the words.

* * * * *

"But why? You do not even know if They exist!"

Yad shrugged. "If they do not, I will find out. If they do, I will find that out, too—and bring back the cone from its head to show."

Narn shuddered slightly. "But They were beautiful. There was a time when They lived with us. They have never done any harm to you."

Yad sighed and shook his head. He knew the words in his friend's heart would challenge what he was trying to say, so his words came easily. "Narn, the Hunters know better. A more fierce beast has never existed. They stalked their victims ruthlessly—"

"No!" Narn was surprised at his own vehemence. "They were beautiful! They lived <u>with</u> us! They caused no harm!" He found himself shaking, his fists beginning to clench. Part of him wondered how this could be when he was wearing the Mask, but it was a part that was less strong than the other parts, and the wondering faded.

"Narn." He leaned on his bow. His dark eyes looked patient. "I would not say these words before anyone else, especially my father. You are my friend. Although I believe you feel I am thick-headed sometimes and do not listen to you, you are wrong. I know how you think, and I do not believe you will be told an unTruth without knowing it. You believe what you were taught, and I believe what I was taught. It may even have once been as you say. But what may have been then is not now. And we are living now. You will not change and that is why I like you. But I will not change either. There are enough stories among the Hunters of the victims run through by the cone of a great one. These stories had to have a beginning. If they still live in the Valley, I will know. I know the walls are not climbable, but the rivers get in. There is a way in. I will find it." Yad said nothing about finding the way to return home. A Hunter did not need talk of that. If the Hunt was successful, the return was the smallest of concerns. If the Hunt was not successful, then the Hunter had not survived and there would also be no need to talk of returning home.

Narn felt a hurt inside, as though a part of him had been destroyed. He was not hearing the words.

* * * * *

Narn was not hearing the words.

"...return, but I will, then you can tell. I must leave now." He looked up at him. Despite the Mask, in his eyes were many unspoken requests. He wanted his friend to remain faithful to his own Lessons. He wanted his friend to know what he knew. He wanted his friend to know what he wished he could say and yet could never say. His eyes spoke many things in the lengthy silence that passed between them. However, by the time the words reached his lips, they little resembled any of that which had been in his eyes. "Wish me—Good Hunt?"

Narn swallowed mentally. His head had in it a fierce buzzing that made quiet the sound of the legendary drisc. There were words in him that needed to be said. There were words in him that must be said. There were words in him that would never be said.

The words that carried the strength fought their way through the barriers before them: those of fear, confusion, and love. The words reached his lips, but found no air there to propel them forth. They called on the lungs to supply them, but the lungs were unsure. They had, indeed, received a request for services. But it had not come from the Hunter, the master—the Man had not exactly told them to work yet. He had been preparing to issue the command, then he hesitated. The lungs were not accustomed to this. A Hunter always gave forth straight, simple commands. This was something new to deal with. For when the Man was the Hunter, he was always in total harmony with himself and with all around him. Yet, here were the words at the lips ready to be spoken, and he had not yet told the lungs to send the air to make the words heard. The lungs knew from past experience the importance of the saying of words in situations and were preparing to request direction from the Hunter. But even as they were readying to ask the Hunter what they should do, they heard the order come and they readily complied.

His voice finally found its way to his lips. "I wish the Hunt—to be profitable," he managed. He was not fully certain he had spoken, although he heard the words on his lips. They were not his choice, they were not what he wanted, but they were all that he could manage. He did not like not having words for his friend. He did not like not being able to be in total Truth with his friend.

Yad smiled knowingly and in a movement that seemed to take forever reached out and clasped the shoulder of the man before him. "I—understand." He nodded and managed a succinct smile. "Truthfully, I could ask no more of you, my friend."

But in that moment, a part of each man reached out and sealed their fondness for each other across time. Beyond their inability to speak in full Truth, beyond anything that might be said by anyone else, beyond their understanding, their friendship was bonded and sealed before the Maker, Who would Honor them at the proper moment.

"Sing, Fabra, sing..."

"Narn?"

"...for tomorrow will come..."

"Narn?"

"...When freedom will ring where..."

"Narn?!"

The song carried a strength of its own and did not want to be stopped from its completion. But there was an interruption, that came repetitively, that was becoming louder than the song as it was sung with all of the things that... The interruption became a voice and it was accompanied by a strong grip on his arm, which was being shaken. His head turned and his eyes looked for the source of the interruption, but saw nothing. His mouth moved, but no sound came out.

The song then faded on its own, and a hollowness was left, a hole that seemed bottomless and unfillable, a space into which everything went and nothing came out, a mouth that swallowed all put into it while the stomach yet hungered, an emptiness that was determined to remain.

"Narn, what is the matter with you? Stop it. You are scaring me."

The voice grew in intensity. It went through him as though it were on a Hunt, skillfully, masterfully. And it found its target, helpless before it. No, not helpless; but strengthless when compared to that which pursued it. The target remained still as the voice came nearer and nearer, almost as though it wished for the Hunt to be ended with it holding no victory. The voice then began to fill the emptiness. The interrupting source took on meaning. And a softness crept into him as stealthfully as the night air creeps upon the sleeper. It was a recognized softness. It was a nice softness. It was a softness that reached into him and left its footprints on the sands of his heart—where they joined the others it had left before.

Before? There was a before? What...?

No, not what, but who?

He spoke again, the words of recognition forming of themselves and this time his ears heard his own words. "Lua? How—"

Her dark eyes were searching his. "Is your heart yet troubled?" The strong grip on his arm remained while a soft hand gently touched his forehead and cheek. "You looked—different."

"I—was." He shuddered momentarily as the Mask also faded, but she did not seem to notice. He looked around. "Where is—Yad?"

She blinked and also looked around, the results of her search producing the same as his. "Yad? Was he here?"

"Yes, he—" The changed length of the shadows on the ground caught his eye. He was silent a moment. Then, as realization came into him and the trail of her voice on his heart moved aside to let the loss be felt, he felt the inner request go out to his heart to beat slowly, to his lungs to breathe deeply, to his face to allow his lips to rise at the corners like they usually did—all so she would not be concerned—and said, "He was, but he—had to leave. I am sorry. I did not hear you come up." The last words sounded in his ears as though they held several meanings, and he wondered which one she would finally hear.

"Yes," she acknowledged, her voice firm, yet soothing. "I noticed that, too. I do not think that has ever happened before." Her eyes narrowed slightly as she tried unsuccessfully to look past the unrecognized expression on his face. "When you did not come back for the meal, I thought you might have had trouble with your arrow points—your Mother told me where to find you."

"That song was going through my mind." He stooped to the ground and began picking up the points he had made. They felt strange in his hand now as though they reminded him of something he was unwilling to remember. He chased off the strangeness, also unwilling to let it be a part of him, and the points became his own again, perfected as he had made them. But they still contained the memory of their last reflections.

"Song?" She knelt beside him and lay an arm over his shoulders, feeling them welcome its embrace. Her arm spoke to her of a stiffness in him that had never been there before. Her heart did not know how to speak to her about this, as there were no Lessons for her to turn to. When her own shoulders grew stiff, she knew their meaning. But in Narn? Did his shoulders speak with the same meaning as hers? His shoulders were not being stiff towards her. They were...as though they were carrying something on them that bowed him down with its weight.

"The one I sang for you by the river the other day," he said, trying to sound rather absent and finding it altogether too easily done. Then his lips were moving again on their own. *"Sing, Fabra, sing..."*

"Yes, it was a very beautiful song. The words were..." She stopped. Something was different in him. It was as though a part of him...was not there, and that there was a...new part of him there that she had never before seen.

"...for tomorrow will come..." "Yes, the words are—very special."

"Narn, your eyes—" As she looked at him, she saw that his eyes were looking, but not seeing. Of a certainty, Narn was there, but he was not there. Something was missing. She was not at all certain she liked how that made her feel.

"When freedom will ring..."

"Do you hear it now?"

"...where the Semsa..." "What?" He turned and looked at, almost through, her. His eyes did not see her. They saw, instead, the music coming to him to be sung...

She did not like that look in his eyes, the one that said she was not there, the one that was not full of her as it had always before been. She pushed him back gently and he fell—no, not fell, but moved, moved slowly—onto the ground. "You hear it now." It did not sound like a question. It was a question, however. She just did not know how to ask something the answer of which she did not know if she wanted to hear. She sat on her knees in front of him, finding a small voice inside her wishing that she had paid more attention to some of the Lessons her Mother had taught her about being with the one Chosen for her by the Maker.

As she was kneeling in front of him, it happened. She filled his eyes, his sky, his mind, his heart—as she once had. In one moment, he reached for the Mask, and in the next, he knew he did not need it—not now, not around her. It was a good thing to know. He wondered briefly why he did not know it more often, why it seemed he knew at one time, and not the next. "Yes. The song—comes and goes. I cannot stop thinking about it." But those words did not satisfy the feeling in him. They did not tell the full Truth that he did not yet understand.

"There is something you are not saying."

"The words mean something." His eyebrows narrowed.

"Well, of course. Why else make a song?"

"But I do not know their meaning."

"You made a song whose words have no meaning?"

"I did not—I did not make it. I heard it only recently for the first time." He shifted, uncomfortably, realizing that he was telling her something that he had kept from her before—and, now, wondering why he had done that.

"Where did you hear it?"

He shook his head, wondering himself as he remembered the first time she had asked him that when they were by the stream. "I do not remember. It is just there."

She pursed her lips, unable to restrain herself further. "Who is Fabra?"

"I do not know." He did not know, and did not know how to answer her more fully.

"She sings."

"So the song says."

"You sing a song about someone you do not know?"

He became silent. His entire body became silent. Even his eyes were silent. The silence in him screamed to be heard.

Lua watched him as she had many times when they were by the river and he would fall asleep and dream. But this was different. She reached out and ran her fingers delicately over his lips. "Think out loud." She had used those words several times with him; they always seemed to give him the freedom to speak that which was held up inside him—for whatever reason.

The sensation that came to his lips at her touch filled them with life, made them cry out to be used as they had been Made. There were words that needed to be said, sounds that needed to be heard, meanings that needed to be felt. His lips parted and a sound came out that was melody.

"Sing, Fabra, sing, for tomorrow will come

"When freedom will ring where the Semsa is from.

"Fly—"

"Narn!" She shook his arm again and the melody stopped. It seemed, though, somehow, that even though the melody stopped, the singing went on—without words.

The shaking traveled through his arm and into his heart and mind. The world before him seemed to shake in answer to the agitation he now experienced. The Sun streaked in its domain. Even the blue of the sky seemed to shudder. Then his entire body lost its silence. He exhaled his next words. "It is powerful."

"Narn, have you—talked with the Mosun about this?" She watched his eyes move as though he was not telling them where to look. She watched as his eyes found hers. In a single moment, they looked into her, deeply. She felt something happen inside her. A feeling came—fleeting, soft and unobtrusive as a night breeze—and her heart began to beat faster. A soft warmth radiated throughout her. It was nice. It was a part of him that she had never before known.

"Lua, I have not even talked with you about this." He felt the warmth return from her and basked in it briefly.

Her mouth opened and then closed. When she spoke, her voice was like the wind that pulled at the morning mists—and trembling.

"You—have never told me that—I mean so much to you."

His eyes regarded hers and they smiled. "Yes, I have."

She felt completely at ease before him now. She also felt completely ignorant. How could he do that? "Then I have been without hearing."

"Maybe so." An impulse ran through him. It was not the first time an impulse had run through him. It was not the first time this particular impulse had found its way into his being. But it was the first time it had come with this strength and also when his thoughts were otherwise already engaged. The impulse took its place in his mind where he made decisions and then directed the necessary commands to the affected parts of his body. It happened so at this point. He leaned over and his lips brushed hers lightly. He felt a shivering hand slide into his. The words came easily, and softly. "You mean so much to me," he whispered. He felt the buzzing in his ears again, and, knowing that the drisc in their supposed land were too far away to be heard, he touched his lips lightly to hers again.

Pictures came into his mind, drawn from thoughts and ideas and desires stored in a special place in his heart dedicated to her. The pictures took on life, fanned the flames of his desires, and lived of their own in him, receiving more strength simply by being allowed to be. The pictures placed themselves over the Truth of the girl before him and caused him to see her in a way that she was not. It was not that she could not be, or that she would not be, or that she did not want to be what he saw. It was simply not her. But the pictures did not care that it was not her. They did not care that they were causing him to see a part of her that was not there. The pictures carried no intended Truth nor unTruth in them. It was not in their purpose to do any of that. They simply were and they simply did as they were Made to do: become more powerful the longer they were looked upon. Thus, intended or not, the unTruth of the pictures grew stronger as he looked at her through them. There were other pictures in his heart that spoke of the wind in the trees, the fliers in the sky, the mists over the Valley... But none of these spoke to him now. He found no desire to look upon them now as he focused on the images of her. So the other pictures did not become strong. Actually, they became far weaker as those of the girl became stronger.

But as the pictures of unTruth became stronger, something else happened deep within him. It was as if an echo was returning when there had been no voice calling to begin it. Somewhere inside him there was a still, small voice whose cries were echoing from his heart with words that had been stored there throughout his entire life. They did not have pictures of their own. They merely were. And with all the strength of the Truth that spawned them, they fought not against flesh and blood—the pictures of the girl—but against the powers of the unTruths contained within those pictures, the powers that could turn his heart cold to the Truth. These words had been written on the tablets of his heart long ago that he might not turn from the ways of the Maker. And as the voiceless echoes reached out for them, they came forth now to fight for and take the place of the pictures.

The pictures of Lua balked. They were there because they had been called by the Man. They were what was wanted. They were what he was enjoying looking at. They were getting stronger because of his desire to look at them more.

But there is order—Truth—in the way in which things were Made by the Maker, and the still small voice speaking that Truth is always stronger than the screaming of any unTruth for those willing to hear it. And Narn was willing now, so the pictures trying to control his mind and heart were not what was best. What was best was known because the Lessons were strong in his heart, and he wanted to follow them. He knew he needed to follow them, even though they were not nearly as pleasant to think on as were the pictures he was seeing of Lua. But these pictures were not supposed to be there at this time in any fashion, even if they were desired. Perhaps later, after their Joining, but not now. Indeed, they were only allowed to continue to exist now because the Man had found them occasionally to his liking and let them be in a particular place in his heart where he might occasionally view them, as it were, from a distance. They were not being destroyed. They were too strong a part of the Man—as they were for most Men. But now they had to retreat back to their cave of silence—until they should be again called upon. There was no longer a place for them here. The Man had decided.

Truth lived.

A feeling of brief embarrassment flushed through him and he wondered if she could sense it. But the thought was too brief to allow for an answer, for he needed to express something more important to her—again. "You mean so much to me," he repeated. "And because so, I will keep my vow." The hand squeezed his, and the pictures once again tried to stand up against his Lessons as though they had the power to make that decision. The thought suddenly came to him that she might be having pictures of her own to deal with, that she was far less strengthened in her decision to fight her pictures, and that her weakness there could seriously affect own strength. "Do not make it so easy for me to take you with less importance."

Her eyes dropped and closed briefly. When they looked up again, they had a depth that was not measurable. Though her own pictures yet screamed at her, she also focused on the Lessons from her Parents, so when the words reached her lips, a partial victory had been won and she spoke only the Truth that made sense, that which she was able to acknowledge while keeping her silence about the flames of her own heart's fires. And so it was that she spoke, for the first time, a portion of the sacred words she had longed to taste on her lips since her eyes were first filled with him. "Narn, my heart—would beat—with yours—"

His mind raced as the words found their recognized place within him, and, hearing them and how close they were to the actual ones to be spoken before their Joining, he realized that she, too, had been having her own battles in her mind and heart with pictures trying to lure her into seeing him in a different way before his time, so he never hesitated as he looked into that depth with his own as the Truth was free to live and knowing that Truth made him free. "And mine with yours.— And they will.— But there are things that I must do first."

She looked back into him now. "I know. But I wanted to hear the words on your lips."

He stood slowly and pulled her up with him, finding that neither of their legs were all that steady at the moment. "There is something I must do now. Come. Have the evening meal with us, and we will enjoy your company."

The two stood together. They were two, then. Not just two separate, but two together. They had been for some time. They had known this. But they had not spoken of it. Lessons forbade that until it was nearer their time for the two to become one. And now, as the time neared for their Joining, the speaking was allowed and they did so. The speaking was not merely the saying of words, but the saying of the words that affirmed what they had known. Saying words from the Lessons that affirmed what one knew was to say that which the Maker had Intended. So there was a strength in them now as they were two together that had never been there before as they were two separate. That strength would be stronger as they became closer to the Maker and, as such, became closer to each other. The only thing that could ever cause a weakening in that strength would be for the eyes of one to not see the Maker as they were Intended, for then they would also not see the other as they were Intended. But for now, both sets of eyes were full of each other—as they were Intended.

That evening, after the meal, they were seated before the fireplace, listening to the song it sang as the small twigs ignited and spread their light and heat to the firelog. Narn had just placed the additional firelog when his Mother chuckled. She was a happy person anyway, but there was something extra happening in her laughter this time. He knew she was about to speak. He remembered how his Father used to prepare to say things to him this way. It would not be simple words. But it would be great words. He prepared himself.

"Narn, what is it you are about to do?"

He glanced at Lua, and then looked at the very old, very loving, very understanding woman. She seldom asked him a question to which she did not already know the answer. His Father used to do that when he was teaching him. But now—?

The knowing eyes sparkled with life, despite their failing in normal sight. "I know you, Narn. You need not pretend with me."

He sighed and nodded as he grouped the tender sparks around the base of the log. "Mother, I will sit atop the Valley tomorrow at lightbreak. Music is in my ears, and I need to sing the melody before the Maker as it comes. He will Give me the meaning."

She chuckled again, looking at, but her failing eyes only seeing the shadow of, the young woman whose eyes were full of him. "Indeed? You see what you can expect, Lua? He dreams and sits on cliffs and listens to music singing in his ears."

Lua turned her face as the familiar smile appeared, but the firelight was bright and it reflected from the side wall and cast a glow on her that only enhanced the beauty of the embarrassment she was trying to hide.

"Mother knows the tamernans will sing their color for us eventually," Narn said to Lua, purposefully watching the glow on her skin become darker and thoroughly enjoying the effect.

His Mother nodded approvingly. "She is rich; therefore, you are the richer, my son."

"I know." He took Lua's hand and pressed it to his lips lightly, feeling it tremble as he did. Then he took his Mother's hand and squeezed them both. "And now, I leave. I will see you soon—tomorrow, perhaps. Good Sleep, Mother."

The aging woman nodded.

"Come, Lua. I will walk you to your Family's Home before I go."

"Good Sleep, Mother-of-Narn," said Lua as softly as she could manage without her voice cracking.

Again, the woman nodded.

At the edge of her Family's ground, they stopped. Lua was looking at their shadows, cast by the Moon. Narn noted them, too, as they played in the firelight cast by the distant main fire for the Village, creating another set of shadows and, for a moment, he pondered what they would have looked like in the light of two Moons.

"What?" He realized she had spoken.

"I said your Mother has accepted me tonight."

"Yes. I knew she would. I told you that."

"But I did not know she would. I did not even know that she knew about—about—how I felt." Briefly, she allowed herself to relish the feelings, and then felt her face become warm. Her first impulse was to turn away and hide the obvious. But as quickly as the warmth had appeared, a comfort then filled her and she looked up into the eyes of Narn and allowed the warmth and the comfort to manifest themselves as one of her smiles.

Narn embraced her. "Lua, it would have been impossible to hide our feelings from her. Her life has been built on love. How could she possibly not recognize it when it is standing there in front of her?"

He felt her suddenly crush herself to him, a move that he found he thoroughly enjoyed, and he had to think about why she had done so to keep his thoughts from wandering again. So it was that he heard both with his ears and his heart.

"You are going away from me."

The Truth of the statement in his ears met its companion in his heart and he accepted it. He also accepted it coming from her. It was good to not have to say some things.

"I will be back." It sounded strong and final on his lips.

"Will you?" She was suddenly very silent and still, as though she had not heard the same words he had just said....or, perhaps, she had not heard them in the same way he had said them.

Narn found himself listening to her. Not only to her breathing and her words echoing in his mind, but to her. She was a mixture of feelings, and rightfully so. But one began to be stronger than the others. It skillfully moved around the others and asserted itself in the foremost of her heart so that she had to feel everything else through it. He had seen it before in others, but never in her. It looked so out of place. It was a blot of lessness on the beauty that was before him, and he wished he could remove it from her. It had a name, and its name was fear. He saw the fear rising in her, trying to assert itself where it was entirely out- of- place, and he suddenly understood and pulled her tightly to him. "Lua, Lua. I will let nothing stand between us. Even the fiery gates of Ha'as will not—" *"Sing, Fabra, sing..."* "Nothing." His voice remained soft while his mind shouted the word, half in fear of scaring away the song forever, and half in fear that it would not retreat at all. "If it is the Maker's will, our hearts," he turned her chin upward and looked into her eyes, "will beat together for always. Nothing can prevent that."

"Not even—Fabra?" She swallowed, not fully understanding her own question.

He regarded her for a moment. There were many things that were not being said by her words. She had been getting better at doing that. He found he enjoyed it. It made him listen all the more to what she was saying. There was purpose here. She feared for him to leave. She feared the meaning of the song that she did not understand. She feared he might not be able to return. Indeed, there was a lot of fear in her at this moment. But then, the Maker did not Write fear into their hearts, so it did not have to be heeded. If so, it was done as a choice. And now he needed to help her make that choice. He accepted her words and their meaning and smiled. "Not even Fabra."

By now she could scarcely hear her own words as the fierce pounding of her heart nearly rendered her ears of no use. The sacred words that would separate her from all other men until the time of their Joining echoed within her and added to the cacophony. She had been saying them over and over for a long time now, trying to find the perfect way to say them to him when the Moment was upon them. And now, as she realized that that time was now, all of her practicing faded away as she barely whispered, "My heart would beat with yours for always."

Narn had been doing his own practicing at hearing the words and giving his own back to her. But the near-suddenness of her speaking those words, all the words—in their intended use—that were so sacred, so pure, so full of what the Maker Intended nearly caught him off balance. Clearly this was not a time for the Mask, but it was obvious his feelings were so strong that they may one day put him in danger if he was in a Hunt. He realized that he would have to learn how to decide much more quickly on the use of the Mask. At this time, however... As his heart beat one more time, he re-directed all his attention on the figure of beauty that the Maker had Placed before him, and he said the words that were the only possible and Truthful response to hers that would accept her apart from all other women until the time of their Joining. "For always has already begun for us." His lips touched hers lightly. He found her suddenly very strong and unwilling to release him from the enclosure of her arms. It was more than the mere embrace that normally came when two people agreed to Join their lives apart from all others. It was more than the embrace that came from the fires that burned within at the nearness of each other. It was if in her encircling him with them, she was trying to protect him from some great danger, something she feared was coming to pull them apart.

And then, as suddenly, she was running to her Family's Home. Once inside, she did not look back, and the door closed.

Narn stood silently looking after her until a sork's cry from overhead made him aware of the loneliness creeping upon him.

X

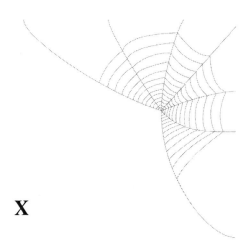

The tamernans swayed and softly sang out their tiny whine along with their mists as the warm breeze found its silent way through them. They reveled in singing their song. They had sung their song since they were Made. They had no other purpose in life than to do that for which they had been Made. It made things simple. There was no Confusion. They all performed their tasks well. And the resultant Intended beauty was a tribute to the Maker.

The water in the small stream continued on its way. It, too, was performing its tasks exactly as it had been Intended. It carried water from one place to another, bringing life and cool sweetness with it. It noted that in one part near the shore, there was something that it had not allowed to be placed there as a result of the gradual weathering away of the shoreline. There was a stone. Since the water did not—could not—pull a stone on its own into its path, a Man must have placed the stone there. And still—on top of it, there was another stone. This, indeed, was not what the water had come to expect. But it did not mind. It did as it was Told, and the forces of it pushing against the stack of rocks finally defeated the forces holding the rocks there, and the stone rolled over into the shimmering liquid with a soft splash.

The figure near the stream stirred, eyes immediately open and scanning the area, one hand already clutching the knife's handle dangling at its waist.

His gaze fell upon the stream where he had placed the small rock, and he smiled and allowed himself to stretch. He felt his muscles welcome the action. They were tight from the orders placed upon them the day before. Indeed, he had needed the nap. He took his knife and dug around the circle of rocks on his left. Their warmth was minimal now, as the firecoals in their midst had long earlier gone out. But the meat set between the rocks was still warm, and he gratefully ate most of it.

Hunting early in the Valley had been rewarding, as expected, and his food pack was now rich with an assortment of sork and v'rill. The v'rill were small, but he expected to find more of them. The stream must eventually empty into a pool for common drinking. There would be families there, and larger targets would make themselves available to him.

He rose and, taking note of the moon about to be eaten by the jagged peaks of the far rim, he set off into the forest along the stream. He wanted to be further in by lightbreak.

Shortly, the stream divided itself. He hesitated and looked down both paths of flowing waters. A good Hunt could usually be found where a stream fed a pool. But both streams now went in near-opposite directions, and this was uncommon, since the landslope was toward the Valley's center. The trees blocked his vision along both, and neither waterpath made any sound. His body listened. His body waited. And he listened and waited.

The tops of the peaks that had devoured the moon began to glow in the familiar lightbreak, and the figure's eyes turned skyward as a faint slicing of air was heard. Indeed, it was very faint, for it was a sork gliding high above the forest, head slightly inclined, its sharp eyes examining the ground. It circled a moment, toying with a wind that was selfish in that it was not reaching the forest. This wind was content to frolic about in the higher airs, sometimes even above the clouds. And, occasionally, it allowed itself to dip down low enough for a venturous sork to enjoy it. This was one of those times. The sork looked down, lifted one wing slightly, and sailed off along the direction of one of the streams.

The figure on the ground smiled. His Hunter's instinct told him that the sork would not fly where there was no food, and he set off along the fork of the stream that the adult flier had followed. His journey, his Hunt, was going to be full of rewards. He felt his heart begin to beat slightly faster and rebuked it silently, internally. He did not need to waste strength on feeling good merely because events were taking place as he had foreseen them in planning the Hunt. There would be plenty of time later when he returned to his home with the results of his Hunt.

As he walked, ensuring he made no sound to alert any enemy—or prey—, his eyes took in the forest through which he was now travelling. The brush had grown thick very quickly, a sign that the water in the area was plentiful and pure. But the sudden thickening of the trees surprised him. As did their shapes. It was as though they were trying to connect the ground to the sky but some great wind kept blowing them back down, keeping them there is their twisted forms. Their branches held no fruit, something else that surprised him, for trees similar to these back in his homeland always gave forth an abundance of fruit...usually enough for the entire tribe and all its families. His fingers told him nothing different about them as he ran them along some of the trunks he past. There was nothing remarkable about them. They were just there.

Sometime later, the gnarled trees fell back and revealed a large open field through which the stream continued. He stood very still and only allowed his eyes to move over the area. And he received his reward. He saw the expected tracks of a family of v'rill. But there were not as many as he had anticipated, and they were scattered all about rather than running in their usual orderly fashion. Normally their families ran closely together, especially when there were going to a watering place. The Hunter allowed his thoughts to consider what he was seeing. Something was here that was not normal. There was something... His instincts spoke to him.

He looked up suddenly and his eyes again surveyed the area. There was nothing there that had not been there before. There was nothing there that should not be there. Was there supposed to be something else there that was not? Had he overlooked something in his eagerness to find the family of v'rill? He looked again. His instincts commanded his eyes to look beyond what they were seeing, to look for the things that were not seen, to keep the Hunter safe. The tamernans had ceased their soft resultant cry. The silence had come upon him also unexpectedly. Usually the hushed cry of the colorful but vulnerable plants carried on as long as there was wind. But...his skin talked to him now. There was also no wind. His instincts reacted to this now, for they had missed when the wind had ceased. Such a failure in his instincts could mean the end of his life. Perhaps he had not spent enough time strengthening them before he came on this Hunt.

No. That was not correct. It was also not true. His instincts were the best of anyone in his tribe. The idea that they might not be as strong as needed was coming from the place in him where his feelings were kept, and apparently the door to that place had been opened by the surprises of the area. Surprises are to be expected in a new land, even when things looked the same as in his homeland. But it did mean he would have to ensure he listened to them well, for they would keep him alive as he faced the things of which he knew not. He stared intently through the lingering mists. They floated on the air with no wind to push them one way or the other, causing a dance with the light from the sun. It was almost as if they were now a part of the air, filling in the blank spaces between the trees, darker in some areas, lighter in others. There was no sound, no movement. There was, indeed, no sign of anything at all that carried life but for himself. And such a scene was never possible, especially when a Hunter was present. There was always life to find, to Hunt. But...there, indeed, were none here.

So something must be wrong with this place. But that decision would be baaed on the way things were in his homeland. What if things here were different? Would his instincts know what their sensings here meant? Would they mean the same as they did back in his homeland? All signs indicated danger, but he sensed none. What had happened to his instincts? What was this place? What was... He cocked his head, and then in one swift action, his bow was off his shoulder and an arrow strung on it, the fingers anxiously awaiting the command to release their familiar playmate.

"Why?" He argued with himself as his fingers retained their tenseness on the bowstring. *"There is no danger."* His Hunter's instincts flashed back warnings. Warnings of nothing where there should be something meant danger. Yet he sensed no need for them to be there. His eyes narrowed. There was disagreement within himself. There was Confusion. There was no balance. Where were his senses? Where was the oneness that needed to be there for the Hunt? The Mask was in place. Indeed, it had been there since he had left the Village. Why did not the Mask— Why did not his senses—

The shadows in the mist faded away as the lightbreak reached them, and the stream that was now visible disappeared silently into the green-tinted cloud.

The figure felt his stomach grow weak. This was not good. It was the oldest of instincts. Strength was stored in the stomach. Strength came from the stomach. It was not that he was experiencing hunger. This was the strength from which his very life lived. And it was weak. What had caused this?

The Hunter continued to ready himself, despite the Confusion that now reigned throughout him. He knew what to do. He done it many times before. He knew how to Hunt even when his instincts were not there. And so he sent the silent commands to his body to prepare. His legs became tense, as did his arms. They were ready for battle. They were responding to the many rigorous years of training to be ready to fight against the danger, against the enemy. And, indeed, they were ready. They were signaling their readiness. The fingers tightened around their weapon. They, too, had had much instruction on preparations for facing danger. They signaled their familiarity, their comfort, their oneness with the weapon. They were poised, ready to face the danger.

He shook his head. What were his instincts telling him now? It was clear that part of him sensed danger while another part of him sensed none. He looked around, ahead, behind—above. He saw nothing that proved menacing. Yet, his instincts continued to tell him that there was something about which to be concerned.

There was no danger. But— there was something. There was...

His feet spoke to him, then his legs, then his torso. The ground reverberated slightly; then the water in the stream rippled. Yet, no sound reached his ears. No animals ran from the bushes. Where was—

The figure's eyes—the Hunter's eyes—searched the floating mist, the mist that had always come from the plants when things were quiet.

And the mist parted.

It came charging at him with a speed that almost rendered only a blur, the gleaming shaft atop the head pointing at him with an infallible accuracy.

The Hunter's senses spoke to him of a mild surprise. The Hunter had experienced surprises before, although not many. Too many would mean he would not be returning from a Hunt. And he had purposed in his heart to not let that happen. However, he agreed with himself that he had not really expected it to be that large. A part of him had not really expected it to be there at all. Indeed, the togrun was dwarfed by the beast. There was little opportunity, however, to allow more time to properly appreciate the enemy. During the single heartbeat that allowed that thought itself, the attacker had closed the space between them.

The Hunter's arms of power tensed in the aiming, his fingers of accuracy relaxed, and his specially-prepared arrow left the bow in an odd silence, drowned out by the thunder approaching. The shaft met the attacking horror only a moment before the Hunter found himself hurtling through the air and becoming engulfed by darkness.

"Bring She life, bring She death?"

Narn shook his head as his eyes gazed sightlessly into the air over the Valley. The light green glow of the tamernans' mist held its color and the depth of that color without wavering. His eyes moved now as they began to look more closely at the things before him. The sky along the rough edges of the distant mountains was preparing to again welcome the Sun. Lightbreak was over. The air should be already have begun its dance so that the song of the Sun could be sung with beauty as it was reflected through the mist. And yet...how was it that the mist still clung to the trees and all the other plants in the Valley?

The things that had been Made for an Intended purpose were not doing what they had always done before. He had watched many lightbreaks, had enjoyed many Moments at this particular time when the Sun reclaimed the sky from the darkness. But each object had its own special part to perform in the scene. And that was not happening. Indeed, as he watched on more closely now, nothing was happening as it should have been. There was a total absence of anything happening at all.

Then it changed.

He felt his heart surge, augment its throb of life to a near-deafening roar, and then he became unaware of its fierce pounding. It was not that the beating of his heart was unimportant. Something else was there. The wind, now moving, pulled at his hair and sought to cool his brow, but he did not notice it. It was not that he did not appreciate the cooling of the wind. Something else was there. His ears now spoke to him of the increasing buzzing that rivaled that of any hopeful drisc, and it became unbearable. It was not that he did not appreciate what his ears were telling him. Something else was there. Before him, his eyes took in all that now moved, all that now changed, and the ways in which they happened that were different from how they were Intended, and he wished for blindness to touch his eyes. But there was nothing he could do to take away what lay before him. For even if he, himself, turned away, his memory would draw the picture again and again. His chest hurt now, from the extra fierce beating of the life-giving heart within it, but it was not enough to distract him. Nothing would distract him now.

For the tamernans were singing and their mists were changing color.

An unseen hand reached through his chest, grabbed his heart, and ripped out a part of it. A loss, an indescribable loss—without words—more than feelings—part of his being. In one instant, the dream of all dreams had come to pass. Knowledge had come. Legends of things only whispered passed and now had been proven. Momentous celebration now had become for always melancholia. With his mind he knew what he knew, and yet, with his heart, he wished he could unknow all that he knew. For in that one moment as he saw the mist change its color, he knew that a Great One lived. Yet, in that same moment, the very thing that had brought his dream into reality had taken it from him, for the tamernans were singing...

His mind reeled and rebelled. At what? A thought? A feeling? A desire? A dream? A memory? A memory of something never had, yet to be remembered? All these and more. A mere word. A word that had once described the beauty of Something Made, the beauty of That Which was Made honoring Its Maker in Its very being. Now a word only. A word that once meant hope for things yet to come would be held in memory as that which was of the utmost pain. A word which would be remembered no more as beauty. A word only.

...topin—

as the Name of the Great One was Called.

Somewhere, somewhen, in a time and place far away from there, a Mother had said the Name of her Little One as the Name had been Given to Her by the Maker. That Name was a real part of the Being from that time forth. That word, that Name would be spoken by the Maker when it was time for that One to return to Him Who had Given it in the first place. But this Name would never again be heard by any ears made of flesh. And it would never be heard by those ears who had only once dreamed of hearing it, of perhaps even hearing it spoken on the lips of their owner. The dream remained; but now, the Name was gone for always.

And then—a new feeling screamed itself into the cacophony within him. His legs wavered. There was more?? The song that sang within him now was no longer the song of oneness with himself. It was no longer the song of harmony that made all things aright. It was no longer the song that he had learned all his life of the Truth of things.

There was a new loss. A new horror. It located with ease the entryway into his heart and found it already filled with the loss of Something for Which he had only dreamed. It struggled at that loss and found it a strong opponent, not at all yielding. It noticed that as long as it struggled to gain a place here, there would be no place made for it, for so great was the other loss that it nearly filled the entire heart. This was unacceptable to the force behind the new loss, for it was as real as the other and it deserved a place of equal feeling. But then—it did not have to have a place of its own in order to have its pain known as much as the other's. It merely had to be for its effect to have purpose. So it was that the strength of its pain joined that of the other.

As the resulting pain of the combined losses augmented, the effect was greater than the sum of them as individuals. The losses did not take pleasure in this. They merely did as they were Intended. They were there to give the individual an opportunity to turn his eyes more toward the Maker than toward the reason for their being there. If they could have felt anything at all, they would have been saddened that so few did just that, but, instead, became consumed with the event that had spawned them in the first place, for the things of the world were Made to bring all other things into oneness with the Maker.

Suddenly, however, without knowing why or how, this new loss for Narn increased, and a loss for something that had been real to him much longer than his recently-fulfilled dreams of Great Ones—this loss began to fill him anew and push back, overshadow, draw out from the earlier loss.

Reality was strong now and although Truth must live, sometimes the Truth of the reality is strong enough of its own that it renders unrecognizable that which once was and that which once was Truth. So the new loss etched itself in vivid colors into his mind, forming another word that would intertwine itself with his soul for always. A word alone is merely a word alone. Its place in the soul of Man gives it the value that it carries as it is remembered, thought, spoken. The word moved upon itself and it took on a name, a name that beckoned to be known. Though the fluids ran down the sides of his mouth as his jaws became closed to the point where they wondered if they would ever again open, the name would not be ignored, and it found its way from his yielding soul to his lips.

"Yad!!!" he screamed, but his voice refused to work.

He closed his eyes that the light of the Sun would no longer shine upon the scene that had blackened his life. And the topin continued. He closed his eyes that they might not see the scene that would for always live again and again in a place where there was now less life. And the topin continued. He closed his eyes that...

A new light came to his eyes, though his eyelids were tightly closed, his fists buried into them that they might accidently open on their own and he again see the topin. And again he wished that sightlessness might touch him, because this light that touched his eyes came from within himself. No matter how he turned his body the light continued to come forth. It began as a small flame seen in the distance, carried, perhaps by a traveler in the darkness. And rather than grow to be brighter on its own, it came towards him, becoming larger as it approached him. And with it came the picture with its own horror that it contained.

Yad lay on the ground, lifeless, emaciated, his life fluids draining from his body.

Narn closed his eyes tighter, but the light would not lessen, the scene would not fade, the loss of life would not be replaced. He pressed his fists harder into his eyes till the colors that came forth nearly rendered him sightless and he felt his awakeness begin to leave him, but the vision was as distinct as ever. "Yad!!!" And still, he could not call out.

His lungs told him they were using air much too fast for the small amount of movement his body was performing. He frantically tried to calm his breathing but there would be no control. He was facing an enemy that knew no defeat, one whose attacks would not be thwarted. So the gasping of air continued. He called upon his Hunter's instincts to put within him the controls of his responses that were needed. The

Mask came unbeckoned, recognizing its need, but even the Mask seemed to have its limitation. It knew that it could not work against something that was as much a part of its owner as it was. It could not work against itself. And so it, too, failed.

His voice told him that it was not able to give him what he felt he needed most at that time, that which was likely the only thing about himself that he could control at that moment. But it found itself not able to respond because of all the air his lungs was using. His ears began to fail him, the whine of the flora long ago lost, the cries of the fliers not heard for some time, all of the things that once brought music to him—all no longer a part of his world. His attempts at crying out became lost in the colors as they made his ears without hearing and his eyes now without seeing. Yet the abhorrence remained.

He wanted the scene to go away. He wanted it to be a bad dream from which he could awaken. He wanted the dream to stop. But there was no awakening. There was no reprieve. The dream was now a part of him that he could not deny. He could feel it coursing through his entire being, each heartbeat making it stronger as he became weaker. It would last as he lasted. It was as real as he was.

And so he wished to not be real. He wanted to not be real, to not have to see or hear anything more. There was not one part of him that did not hurt now, and he wanted to not have to face anymore hurt, anymore badness. He wanted to let the empty feeling in his stomach be that which filled it. He wanted to let the empty feeling in his mind be that upon which he would focus his thoughts. He wanted to let the empty feeling in him be—him. Indeed, if there was only emptiness in him, there would no longer even be hurt there to remind him of what he had lost.

But Truth is a powerful thing. And when one has had the Truth in him for so long, a battle will rage when the Truth is told it must leave. And so it was, that a new battle raged inside the mind and heart of the demeaning figure on the precipice. It was a battle that would continue to the final end, even though that end may not be for a long time. So in the meantime, the figure would do whatever he needed to do to try to lessen the terrible hurts he was feeling.

To not be real would be to not have Truth, and to not have Truth would be to have unTruth. And only the Truth could make you free. And Truth must live, so he needed to want to be real, even though everything inside him screamed out the need to be otherwise. He needed to want to be. But there were other needs. Needs that were now foremost in his being because of his losses. He needed to be real to have the Truth. But even more, he needed... He needed... He wanted... He wanted...

...his friend.

And an entirely new feeling came to him. It began as a small, unimposing, unthreatening sensation. It gently nudged its way past his Lessons, past his defenses, past his heart and, as a seed, took root in his mind. And in that place a coldness crept it. But it was more than cold: it was an extreme absence of warmth. There was no heat, nor light in it, and it sucked the life from everything around it, leaving only blackened, charred ground in which there could be no growth. It then moved quickly into his heart, following the life fluids throughout their journeys into every part of him and back into his heart—leaving its trail of blackness, of lifelessness throughout him. Part of him, a diminutive fraction hardly noticeable in the blackened portion, seemed to cry out something, something that sounded vaguely familiar, something that did not quite agree with all that was happening within him. But it proved no match for the attacking lifelessness and was quickly lost in the mass of blackness now filling him. He did not exactly like the feeling, even though it seemed perfectly comfortable inside him. But it seemed to be giving him little choice as to its presence. It was unwilling to move from its new home, and he was now too weak to demand otherwise. So he chose to let it remain, and it became a part of him and would affect all of his thoughts and feelings after that.

When true sight returned to his eyes, Narn became aware of the throbbing pain in his uplifted hands. His fists were still tightly clenched, the nails digging deeply into his palms, spilling red down his arms. They were shaking uncontrollably. His entire body was trembling and wracked with waves of fiery pain. Then everything became blurred as the water flowed freely from his eyes, and he slumped to the ground, still unable to make a sound. *"You were right,"* echoed through his mind from his heart, not coming from him but from within him as though the words were not his own. But since they said what he had wanted to say, he accepted them as his own...and so they became. His breaths now came in short gasps, and as one blackness attacked his sight from all sides, another blackness closed in over him and through him, obscuring any remembrance of his Father's words and the Lessons therein.

XI

As he moved doggedly among the brush, sight slowly returned to his eyes and thinking gradually came again to his mind. There were branches slapping against his body as he pushed through them. Some left small welts on him. Some did not. They were not viewed as threats to him. They were simply acting as they always had. Some were crushed under his feet. Some sprang back up. Some did not. They were not viewed as threats. They were simply acting as they always had. The brush was thick. It obviously had a good water supply. However, it normally did not take this much effort for him to move among the wildness of the growth. Perhaps it was due to the overall tiredness he noticed pulling at his own limbs that was the cause of the hampering of his forward movement. Perhaps... One eye took note of a particular plant as he pushed its branches out of his way and proceeded past it. And its strangeness called out to him. It was not a plant that was immediately familiar to him. He stopped now and looked all around him. There were some trees that were of those which grew near his Home. Their fruit was clearly known to him. But here...and over there... Those trees... Their bark did not have... And those bushes... He looked at them now more closely. They were not known to him, yet he had seen them before.

His memory began to draw pictures and he realized he had, in fact, seen them before. But they were smaller. Much smaller, indeed. Smaller? How could a tree be smaller? The pictures in his mind continued. Smaller. Yes. Because they were seen—from a distance. A great distance with them far below him. Below? His gaze continued up past the trees and he saw in the distance behind him and to the sides harsh walls of the area in which he now found himself. Yes, he knew this place. Although he had never been here. He had viewed it many times from a distance—as he sat on the top of those walls. He was now actually in the Valley, his knife in its attack sheath at his waist, his holder of special arrows over his shoulder, and his Hunting bow in his hand. Looking briefly again over his shoulder to the walls distant behind him, he found he did not remember the descent down their jagged edges; and he also found, despite the new bruises on his knees and legs, that he did not care. If he was to get out, he would find the way. He had found the way in. He had been told by the best Hunter in the Village—likely in the entire land— that his skills equaled, if not surpassed, his own. They would, therefore, be used. As that thought filled him, he found his fingers closing more tightly on the bow without telling them to do so. The bow had been constructed so as to fit perfectly in the hand of the owner, but there was something more now, something that made it seem to fit more absolutely, as though the bow and the hand of the owner had come from the same construction, cut from the same tree, made for the same purpose. And so it was. They would act as one.

Nearing a stream, his stomach spoke to him harshly, reminding him of his inattention to it, that he needed to serve it in order for it to serve him. He pushed aside the thoughts and pressed on through the foliage, putting his thoughts only on that which lay... The pangs of hunger lashed out again, and Narn found it necessary to reaffirm the vow whose words found no place in his memory but were part of him all the same. "Not until I avenge my friend will I taste food again." And then, from deep within came other words, the ones as though not his own, the ones that came from the blackness that had filled him, the ones that had a life of their own even though they carried lifelessness. These words found their way to his lips and were bitter as they were tasted, leaving bitterness where they had been. "Yad was right!"

The affirmation burned within him, strengthening itself and the feelings that went with it. Although the feelings were new to him, they had become a part of him and they now thrived within him in the blackness that lived where there had once been light. With every moment that the feelings persisted, they grew stronger and easier to hold onto. As their strength increased, they took advantage of the lack of strength around them, in the paths whereon they had walked, and they began to reach into every part of him, seeking out those places of hidden feelings, hidden Lessons that would oppose their existence. As they found them, they quickly, skillfully, masterfully moved around them, not disturbing them. The affirmations knew that these earlier Lessons were very powerful and that they could never be destroyed. But they also knew that these Lessons could be separated, sealed off so they could not be reached, not be used, not be felt as long as they, the affirmations themselves, were being used. And the longer they could make this happen, the weaker would be the effects of those Lessons. They were determined to live within him. For the will of the blackness that sent them was very strong.

As his teeth seemed to clench themselves, his stride lengthened. He must go faster. There was an urgency. He did not question it. It merely was. He did not question what was. It would use valuable strength that would be needed for the battle with the enemy. Water then blurred his eyes, and he blinked it away with a new fury. There was no place for it now. It would also use valuable strength that would be needed for the battle. His grip tightened again on the bow. The string on it had been especially spun to give the bow extra power to bring down quickly any adversary he might meet on a Hunt. It would be used now, although not in the way he had originally intended it.

"No!" He threw the thought from his mind. Intent mattered not! A bow was used to take life, and so it would! It would do what it was supposed to do, and it would do it with a purpose that now burned within him! Earlier ideas were unimportant. Only the now could be. And the now said that there was only one purpose. And he would see that purpose take place! The affirmation grew stronger and buried itself even deeper within him, and the words came to him again which were slowly becoming a part of him. Yad had been right!!

By the time the Sun was disappearing behind the rim's peaks, Narn was lying beside a stream that disappeared into a forest of trees whose twisted frames and misshapen trunks made him realize that the trees he used to so often play in near the edge of his land were of a similar nature. The shapes beckoned to him, though the warm wind had long since ceased her journey through the leaves. A memory of the trees at Home found its way past the feelings, past the affirmations, and it lived in him for the moment. The affirmations were caught off guard and had no choice but to let the memory live. To move so directly against something that had been so great a part of him would be to give themselves away. They knew that, like all memories, this one would fade in time. And they would still be there.

And Narn felt a hurt inside.

* * * * *

"But why? You do not even know if They exist!"

Yad shrugged. "If they do not, I will find out. If they do, I will find that out, too—and bring back the cone from its head to show."

Narn shuddered slightly. "But They were beautiful. There was a time when They lived with us. They have never done any harm to you."

Yad sighed and shook his head. "Narn, the Hunters know better. A more fierce animal has never existed. They stalked their victims ruthlessly—"

"No!" Narn was surprised at his own vehemence. "They were beautiful! They lived <u>with</u> us! They caused no harm!" He found himself shaking.

"Narn." He leaned on his bow. His dark eyes looked patient. "I would not say these words before my father. You are my friend. I know how you think, and I do not believe you will be told an untruth without knowing it. You believe what you were taught, and I believe what I was taught. It may even have once been as you say. But then is not now. You will not change and that is why I like you. But I will not change either. There are enough stories among the Hunters of the victims run through by the cone of a great one. These stories had to have a beginning. If they still live in the Valley, I will know. I know the walls are not climbable, but the rivers get in. There is a way in, and there is a way out. I will find them."

Narn felt a hurt inside, as though a part of him had been destroyed.

* * * * *

Narn felt a hurt inside, as though a part of him had been destroyed. His fist had earth clenched tightly in it. He threw it into the stream, and as it sent obscurity through the clear flowing liquid, he closed his eyes wishing for obscurity to come to—

The affirmations moved now.

No. Not obscurity. Alertness! Obscurity was only for those who had something to blot out. He was a Hunter and would use all of his senses in this Hunt! He did not need to obscure anything! Everything was as it should be, and he would use everything to help him finish the Journey he had begun. The Hunt would go on! The affirmation claimed more territory in his heart. The words came again. They were a part of him now. They were easy to think, to say. They were real. Yad was right!! "Yad was right!"

Rest did not come easy, but his Hunter's instinct warned him of the need to be fully rested in order to continue the Hunt and be successful. And he would continue.

He resolved to rest.

XII

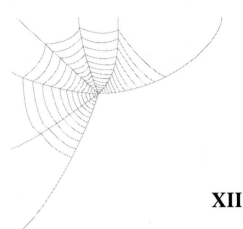

When he opened his eyes, there was no light in the sky, save that of the specks of colored fire whose pictures no longer held meaning for him and whose songs no longer sang for him, and there was water running gently over his left hand. He yawned sleepily and brought some to his mouth. Its cool sweetness refreshed him and he wiped the hand over his face. As he brought his arm up to dry his face, his eyes fell on the other side of the stream. The forest was gone and the stream ran into a pool.

His eyes narrowed, and he strained to see in the darkness. Where had the trees gone?

Sleep left him as his heartbeat echoed the Confusion that now filled him. When he had closed his eyes, there had been trees across the stream. Now... What was happening? Had he traveled again while asleep? But how far had he come? Where— The Hunter felt the Confusion trying to control him.

Confusion exists because it asks the question that does not want to be answered. It asks what the Lesson is that needs to be followed in a given situation. Confusion may exist only as long as there is no answer to its question—or as long as the owner will not hear the answer. Confusion is a distracter for a Hunter, and, therefore, cannot be allowed to go on once it has been noticed. The Confusion was then added to its place in the Hunter's thoughts and feelings to be used for strength to prepare to face the enemy. The Confusion did not try to run from its conqueror. It obediently followed the commands given to it. It would have also allowed itself to be commanded to the place of answers. But the Hunter was not currently seeking for the type of answers which lived in that place. So the Confusion remained, and the question remained—unanswered.

There seemed to be movement at the edge of the pool. He lay motionless as his night vision grew and he saw that there were two pack-animals drinking from the pool. A Mother and her child, he suspected. They must have come from the forest—

Forest?...

—well, they came from some place to this pool to drink. From the other tracks he could make out in the ground, this was a popular drinking place. He watched as they drank their fill, then lay by the water's edge. A Mother and her child. There was something—something special about that...something that made feelings come to him...

A quiet floated in the air and entered him. It was a natural thing. Narn had always let quietness enter him, even when he was living as a Hunter. So it was natural now that it should enter him. It happened so quickly that the blackness affirmations of earlier were caught off-guard and had no chance to resist. The areas around them that they controlled became less dark. This, however, did not disturb the blackness affirmations. They knew the areas they were on were solidly theirs. They had been claiming all the areas around them, as well, even though they really had no True hold on them. Now it appeared they would no longer be able to claim what was not theirs. But they knew patience—they had had to be patient before, many times. So they would simply wait in the areas they now controlled for the time to reassert themselves. The time would come again. It had before. They knew this. And so they would wait for that time.

A Hunter is always aware of what is happening around him and within him—unless there is something stronger or more skilled than he that is preventing him from being so aware. The blackness affirmations had been around a long time as had their source. They did not want the Hunter to be aware of their presence, nor their absence. So their withdrawal was quiet and without attention. And, thus, the change was imperceptible to the Hunter.

He closed his eyes briefly and inhaled.

The air was fresh and sweet and full of something else that permeated all around. Loving. There was something special, very loving about a Mother caring for her young. It filled him. Memories sung to him of a time when he had been cared for by his Mother. He exhaled and suddenly caught himself and caused the air to go out slowly and quietly. He did not want to ruin the quietness of the scene, nor alert an enemy that might be nearby.

And the quiet was filled with music. Nature sang, and he enjoyed it when she did. It was as if the melody was carried by the wind that had returned to the trees, among the tamernans, and to the stream. It was the feeling of a Belongingness he used to know, one that—

"Sing, Fabra, sing, for tomorrow will come..."

—one that—somehow—seemed—

"...When freedom will ring where the Semsa is from..."

—familiar!

He felt as though his head were spinning, or perhaps everything about him was spinning. He shook himself—gently, so as not to disturb the quiet, and felt his neck become weak. He had felt his head be heavy before with the need for sleep when he had returned from a long journey or had been working in the fields throughout the night. But this heaviness...

"...Fly with the sork and see with his eyes..."

His eyes opened. The song was in his ears this time, and it seemed to come from the direction of the animals. He squinted in a vain attempt to see more of the scene. However, he did not seem to notice the fierce buzzing that had accompanied the song in the past. It was, indeed, no longer there. Its absence did not attract him. It was merely a fact that would be looked upon later, perhaps. Right now, it was not an important fact in view of the others that were in front of him.

"...Of the choice at the fork and the stopping of cries..."

It became easier to see as he waited. His night-vision must be coming into... Then he realized that it was actually lighter. *"The Moon should be rising by now,"* he thought. *"It would be just beyond the far rim."* He glanced in that direction momentarily to reaffirm his conclusion and saw that, indeed, the Moon had risen. But his eyes went back to the rim as more light was coming from beyond it. His insides jerked of their own, and his mind struggled for a picture to compare with this one, but found none.

In the Moment, when the Hunter is being aware of all things around and within him, he may suddenly find something that does not already have a picture of it drawn in his mind, and a picture forms there as he takes in all that he experiences of that new thing. Then he compares it with things that are similar to it. In the few times that something totally unfamiliar comes to the Hunter, he allows himself only a cursory time span to learn all he can about whatever it is that is facing him so he can determine if it is a threat to him. If so, his body prepares for battle. If not, his body remains at rest. In this Moment there was actually something with which to compare. However, it had never before been compared, and that fact was bringing about feelings within the Hunter that were also new. He took this all in between heart-beats, for this was something he must look upon and decide about quickly.

As he tried to focus on the distant rim, his eyes squinted now—but not from the bright light—as a second Moon rose.

"By the hand of the Maker!" He mentally blinked away the new buzzing that exploded inside his head as the words hissed through his teeth in a combination of fear, disbelief, and something else, indefinable. The second Moon was nearly the same size as the one he knew, but its surface was not as bright and had fewer markings. Between the two, where their light joined, it was nearly too bright to look upon directly. Yet he continued to stare at them as his heart tried to pound through his chest. It received no direct instructions to slow nor lessen its movements, so it continued. The Hunter may need the power it could supply.

A movement by the pool attracted his attention. The Hunter immediately chastised himself quietly in allowing himself to be so affected by the scene with the Moons. His voice had startled the animals and they had stood abruptly and were looking his way. But his eyes, straining again with renewed night blindness, were not fastened on the animals themselves, but on the reflection of light above their heads. Each One had a cone protruding from Its head and gleaming in the Moons' light.

Fear was replaced with panic, disbelief with discontinuity, and the unnamed emotion remained, now strengthened. His mind cried out to run, use his bow, do anything, but his body seemed not to hear the directives and grew even more rigid. The Hunter looked on in awe, since there was no experience for this with which to compare. How did one prepare to fight a dream, especially a dream that clearly had all the killing skills about which his friend had told him. He watched in terror as the smaller One lowered Its head and pawed the ground slightly with one hoof, Its cone pointing at him. Suddenly, It moved and became a blur of deadly gleaming silver- white charging at him. No, not quite...silver-white...but—and here, his heart stopped its beating totally for two beats before it dare beat again for fear it would burst through his chest—topin!

The larger One was as quickly standing on Its hind legs, Its shadow in the Moons' light extending faster than the smaller One moved. Its powerful forelegs tore at the air momentarily as Its mouth opened, and the silence was shattered by the musical cry that came forth and bounced back again from all sides of the trees and the pool.

"Fabra!!"

The small charging blur stopped as though affixed to the ground. It eyed him for a moment, then turned and pranced back to the edge of the pool. The larger One bent low and nuzzled the side of the little One and pushed It behind Itself. Then It looked up and regarded Narn.

Narn felt something happen inside him as the eyes of the Great One looked at him. Something stronger was there than the things inside him that beckoned to him. Something stronger was there than the things of which he knew not. Something stronger was there than the feelings that called to him to act. Even at that distance, even in the dull light they spoke of something that was hidden deep within him. And as they spoke, the things hidden began to come out.

The blackness affirmations sensed this and recognized that this was their last chance to stop the return to his former thinking, putting an end, for now, to their existence and their hold on him. To come out directly into the open against these returning feelings would be to give themselves away and perhaps lose all they had gained by their quiet, patient actions. But they were strong, and they knew that they could always come to him again when given the proper opportunity—they would not remain in hiding forever. And they knew that the opportunity would always eventually come. So a war raged between heartbeats.

He looked at the gigantic creature standing there passively regarding him as Its young One returned to It. Words with his Father came to him. Words with the Mosun came to him. Words with Lua came to him. His own words came to him. This was the assurance of a dream. This was all that he had—

The blackness affirmations gave one last push with these memories. They skillfully noted which area was freshest, had most recently been attained, and would be the easiest to attack. The areas around them began to darken again as they touched certain areas of his mind and heart...and he remembered.

No, it was more. Much more. There had been much—MUCH—hurt. This was that which had caused him so much grief! This was that which had given his heart so much loss! The loss renewed itself with strength more so than before. It was afresh. His heart exploded again with the hurt than had subsided only a moment ago. Now! With their last chance, the hurt moved quickly through his being and went to his seeing. His eyes saw the two creatures differently. This was that which had taken away his friend! He would never again see his friend! He would never again talk with his friend! He would never again spend time in deep discussions, learning! His friend! His friend!! Yad!! Yad was gone!!

* * * * *

"But why? You do not even know if They exist!"

Yad shrugged. "If they do not, I will find out. If they do, I will find that out, too."

* * * * *

He breathed. The air was real. So were the feelings. And the latter filled him as did the air. While the air filled his lungs, giving power to other parts of his body to fight the enemy, the feelings filled his heart and soul and mind, giving power to that which would fight the Lessons of his past.

His dreams were real. His Father's words were...

Yad had been real. Their friendship had been real.

The blackness affirmations saw their chance growing and stood taller. They had not expected it to come so soon, but were delighted that they were made stronger by what he did in his weakness. In his frailty, then, they became more dynamic because he chose to look at what they offered rather than that of his Lessons. Their blackness shielded the Light in him, and the Lessons that had come to him grew faint in their shadow.

The hurt returned. Memories returned, unbidden, and the blackness affirmations came forth, now safely, from their hiding places and lived again freely.

The eyes of the Great One blinked slowly, purposefully. They were looking at him. They were seeing more than him. They were looking right through him, into him, and back again. The gaze would have hurt—should have hurt—had it been someone else looking at him that way. No one had ever looked at him that way. What did It see? Why was It looking at him that way? What was...

But then the great head lowered and turned away. There was

something about that movement that tried to speak a last word to Narn, as the last cry of a flier in the higher skies before the song of the Sun is sung at lightbreak, as the last wind breathes across the field grass at lightfall,—but the blackness affirmations stamped it out as quickly as it came in.

His jaws clamped together, and, as his hand closed on the knife handle at his waist, he felt a fierce fatigue pull at him. It seemed as though his entire body was being pulled apart from within, as though he alone had hauled all the firelogs from the cutting place to his Home. All of his motions became sluggish and it seemed as though he could barely move. The scene blurred before him as though he had been swimming under water. He shook his head to clear it.

When he looked again, The Great Ones were gone and he was alone.

The aloneness hit him. He was truly alone now, as the blackness affirmations had seen to it that he could not feel the oneness of all that was about him. It was not a feeling that was good. He did not like having such a feeling. He felt as though a part of him had been lost, destroyed.

He became a complete creature again, but even in the completeness was Confusion. The Confusion lived because the answer had not yet been accepted to its question. He blinked hard and opened his eyes widely. His night vision was not working as before. What was wrong? It seemed to be darker. He scanned the area quickly. It was definitely harder to see. It was, he was coming to realize, more than mere returned night blindness. His acute senses were returning. His eyes were fine. There was no problem with his seeing. It was truly darker. He looked to the ground and the buzzing that came unbeckoned and screaming into his head deafened the pounding of his heart as his eyes found only one shadow.

One? Where before there had been two?

Two?

One?

The ground on which that single shadow lived was suddenly rushing up to meet him and he let it catch him as his eyes turned skyward, the dwindling light of only one Moon coming through them as they closed with the ground catching him.

XIII

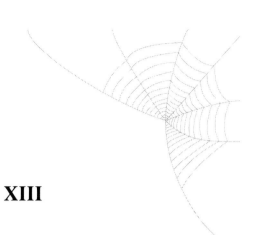

When he opened his eyes, there was no light in the sky, save that of the specks of colored fire whose pictures no longer held meaning for him and whose songs no longer sang for him, and there was water running gently over his left hand. He yawned sleepily and brought some to his mouth. Its cool sweetness refreshed him and he wiped the hand over his face. As he brought his arm up to dry his face, his eyes fell on the other side of the stream—on the forest. Something in the back of his mind cried out to him, and he grabbed for his knife. It was gone. His hands groped frantically over the ground in the darkness until they found it lying by the bank. But the trained fingers did not recognize it. Its blade was well worn, pitted and weathered, and—old; very old. He sat down hard. The grass was soft, but not soft enough to prevent his backside from aching from that movement. He turned the knife over in his hands, straining to see it in the light from the starry sky. He knew the handle. It was the carved Hunter knife his Father had made for him. He had since put in two more blades due to its frequent use. It, too, felt worn and scarred. *"But I just sharpened it in the Village,"* his thoughts ran faintly. *"I*

feel no different." His hand caressed his face and found no more beard than usual. *"I am no older— but my knife— I just sharpened it. And now—it is older than when my Father first gave it to me!"* He ran his hand through his coarse hair and squeezed the back of his neck where an aching was now making itself known. Something was missing.

He looked up sharply as the area began to brighten. Something in the back of his mind cried to him again, and he watched in an unnamed, but augmenting emotion as the Moon continued to rise rapidly. Was it fear? But...why would he fear the sky? The sky had always been his friend, showed him how to find his way when lost, told him of the coming of the seasons. He had never before feared anything in the sky. Why now? No answer came to him. So the Confusion continued to thrive. He found himself staring intently at the far rim, his breaths very shallow. Why? What was wrong? What were his breaths preparing him for? He listened to the parts of him that used to tell him what was happening, what he should do in a certain situation. His feelings were mute. What were they screaming to tell him with their silence? The rise of the Moon had always been one of his favorite times. What had changed while he slept? Was it something in the sky or in the Valley—or was it in him? His eyes moved over the area again, searchingly, and came to rest on his well-formed shadow. Nothing seemed out of place now.

Now?

As he looked down at his shadow in the light of the Moon, the thought came to him momentarily again about what his shadow must have looked like when there were...

...two Moons!!!

Narn jumped up, still clutching his knife and looking at the singular Moon retreating from the teeth of the rim. He found his eyes involuntarily follow the stream as it disappeared into the forest. The forest. It was there.

Of course it was there. Where would it have gone? Forests do not go away. And, still, the Confusion flourished.

His instincts prevailed and his legs became rigid, prepared to... For what were they prepared? There was no...pool. Pool? Why had he thought about a pool? Granted, the pictures in his mind of his experience told him there should have been one there, but why had he looked for it as though... What were his instincts causing him to so intently be looking for? There was no...movement. Movement? Movement of...what? Was there movement? No. There was no movement.

This time. This time? Had there been? Had movement been there? Whose was it? Why did he look for...them? Them? Them? Who were...they? Confusion fed well on his lack of answers and left a taste in him that was unappealing. He disliked having no answers to the questions of his surroundings. A good Hunter...

From a time far away, from a place far away, from a cave deep within him, something said that it should be Them and Their movement, not them and their movement.

Why had he thought that? He saw no pictures. There was no Hunter sense that told him this. Whose words were these? Something was missing. His eyes came again to his shadow. It was alone. It was natural. It should be alone. His eyes again searched the area. He was alone. He should be. There was nothing wrong. There was no danger.

No danger? Why had he thought about danger at all? What was this place?

A wrinkle formed in his forehead as he regarded the crusted knife in the glow of the Moon. The instinct had not been right: there was no danger. There was something wrong. It had never been wrong before, even when he was learning. He had always known where his knife was. It was all he had to protect himself. The instinct had told him to reach for his knife when it was not there. But—he did not remember removing it from its sheath, so perhaps the instinct also did not know it was gone. But instincts were to know things that he could never know. That is why the Hunter relied upon them. And so he had. But his knife... It had been out of its sheath. He never took it out unless he intended to use it. Perhaps it had fallen out when...

He searched, but emptiness and the rapid fading of an undefined feeling were his only answer. His fingers lovingly inspected the knife again as did his eyes. Again, no pictures came to his mind to answer the questions formed there. Confusion was strong now. It was, indeed, his knife. It was, indeed, full of agedness that had not been there when he began his Journey— when he lay down to sleep. Sleep. He would not have had his knife out in his sleep. A Hunter always kept it... Again, only emptiness answered the questions that were now fading in his mind. Questions that...

Questions that...

There was something else there besides the questions. Something...

The blackness affirmations again saw their opportunity and beckoned. It was time to let the Confusion do its work for them. And so the Confusion spoke to the Hunter, to Narn—to Narn, the Hunter. It reminded him of the questions and how important were their answers. But, here, it took on a new approach and allowed in the idea that the importance would not decrease with the passage of time. There were other things that were important for him to concentrate on.

Yes, he realized. There were questions. Questions, however, that could be answered some other time. He was not here to answer questions! There was a Journey to complete! Only then would his questions be answered.

Sheathing his knife, he picked up his bow and set off determinedly into the forest after the stream. The twisted trunks reached out for him, their branches leaving welts on his arms and legs that went unheeded. His time in the forests of his land had been well spent, yet his path went slowly through the denseness of these unfamiliar growths and shapes.

There was a time when the shapes would tell him things about the time of the seasons, what type of fruit they carried, what type of animal liked to eat of its fruit. But these told him nothing. He found he disliked not being able to learn from these trees. Perhaps it was because they were new to him and he just did not understand how they spoke. Perhaps they did not speak at all. No. That was wrong. All things which were Made spoke. The Hunters merely needed to be able to hear them. So, then, where was the cause of the Confusion? The Hunter pressed on.

Abruptly, the scene changed and the trees fell back somewhat to reveal the single stream become two streams, upon which danced the reflected Moon and brighter stars. Both silent paths of water disappeared in near-opposite directions, back into the forest. Narn's arms fell to his sides. He knew a Hunter would always follow a waterpath to find food, but now—

He sat down gently on the soft coat of green that grew along the sides of the stream and let his thoughts focus on Yad. He felt a soft warm wind caress his face and then heard it move through the tamernans that lined the forest's edge. As he listened, a picture was drawn in his mind. Yad. Yad was the best Hunter in the land. How would Yad have chosen?

"Sing, Fabra, sing, for tomorrow will come..."

The picture blurred and began to fade.

"...When freedom will ring where the Semsa is from..."

The blackness affirmations balked, retreated, unsure of what to make of, or how to face this new barrage of feelings. They had seemed to come from nowhere. These feelings did not have ground apportioned to them. How was it, then, that the feelings contained such power? Where was their source? How could the affirmations fight something of which they did not know the source? Clearly, the source of the feelings was other than that of the affirmations, for the affirmations did not fight themselves. But what to do... If they did not act quickly, all they had gained would be lost.

He felt relaxation flood through his mind, though his body tensed, and the picture faded completely. No others replaced it. There was total rest within him for the moment. There was a stillness beginning to fill him like...what used to come during his Quiet. His eyes opened, yet there was still nothing to see.

"...Fly with the sork and see with his eyes

"Of the choice at the fork and the stopping of cries..."

The affirmations attacked anew, lashing out almost carelessly into the Light from their blackness, for they knew they could not let the Quiet continue. It was, they now saw, their main Adversary, and He had appeared suddenly, without warning. There had been no indication that He was anywhere close. They had thought Him lost among the blackened areas. He certainly had been placed there at one time. How had He managed to escape? How could He be so strong after His last defeat? Now they could not be as delicate. There was a certain desperation about them. The Quiet that their Adversary Brought was somehow now more powerful, more forceful than they and would easily displace them if they did not act quickly and shield the Hunter from it.

The darkness, the blackness, lashed out at the Light, and understood It not. So there was no immediate effect; for the darkness, the blackness, then would have to flee from the Light. Unless...

His heart suddenly was pounding in his ears. He blinked rapidly and shook his head as a single picture began to fill and overpower him. It had not come at his request. He really did not know where it had come from, but it was very strong and he needed something strong right then in which to sink his teeth so that there would be no more loss. It was not time to be still. There was no room for Quiet now! Not now!! Quiet only served to let one think on the way things were and how he fitted in with them. He already knew that. He was focused. He was here for a single purpose.

The blackness affirmations, amazed at the seemingly reinforcement of their position in the Man, stood taller now. They would use whatever opportunity they had to dissuade him from listening to anything that would allow him to stray from their path again and seek the Quiet. The purpose was clear,

The purpose was clear. The unbeckoned memory picture of Yad now filled him again. Yad was his friend.

Yad was lifeless. How could someone who is lifeless continue to be a friend?

"Noooooo!!!! He is still my friend!!!"

He must avenge his friend!! There must be only one picture of purpose in the mind of the Hunter! The picture could not come in the Quiet, for the Quiet could not be where such a picture was. And he desired the picture more than he desired the Quiet, so the Quiet had to become less and its lessening allowed the blackness affirmations and the picture to become his focus.

And his picture came.

"*Yad!!*"

The song grew soft and went away, but no other pictures, nor songs, replaced it. He turned his unhearing ears inward and found that the single purpose was there. And that was all that the ears heard. It was all that they needed to hear. He turned his unseeing eyes to the sky and found the single purpose was there. And that was all that the eyes saw. It was all that they needed to see. The eyes found the lonely, single Moon looking back at him. And it blinked.

A shiver reverberated through him. What was—

The Moon blinked again, and he watched. There was nothing to see but the Moon and the light it sang to the Earth. Only—

His ears quickened again. The air above him was moving. His eyes suddenly desired to see and now strained against the Moon's light, until he realized that the sky was growing brighter. And the blinking was a silhouette, which was becoming easier to see. It almost seemed—

A picture came to him. The darkness affirmations were careful to only allow the picture of what he needed to see toward their ends. They would lead him where he needed to go. And so recognition came to him.

A sork! It was circling overhead, its path sometimes crossing the Moon, and so the Moon appeared to blink. At this distance, it would have to be...the largest sork he had ever seen! Its wingspan must be wider than two men standing beside each other with their arms extended out. Where could such a one nest that one had ever seen it before? Narn's hand went to his knife. He had never known a sork, or any flier for that matter, to attack a man. Their food was mostly v'rill. But here, in the Valley—nothing acted in the ways to which he was familiar. And this one was so huge! Maybe...

The flier was suddenly no longer a shadow as lightbreak struck its colors. Narn found himself not breathing, his breath virtually caught in his throat as he marveled at their brilliance. How could such a huge and vibrant creature be so illusive during a Hunt? And yet, it was often so. While the sork often lead Hunters to other foods, they were seldom the catch. Many an arrow had been lost in trying to bring down one of these fliers. And, in doing so, many Hunts had gone on unsuccessful. The Hunters now seldom tried to bring one of these to the dinner table unless there was a special event occurring of which they wanted to celebrate in the feasting of a larger meal. The sork was sailing on in an elegance of its own when it suddenly lifted a wing slightly, the only movement Narn had seen, and glided off on a path that paralleled one of the streams.

Narn's mouth relaxed slightly and a smile almost crossed it. No attack—this time. Perhaps not all thing in the Valley were different from his Home. He let the knife fall back into its sheath.

An echo...

The blackness affirmations were not sure now. To keep silent would be to hold to the picture he had and to let the song be sung. To come forth again would be to silence the song and to allow the picture to fade and be replaced by the Quiet. They had, now, their own sense of Confusion. They did not want to lose any more of their battle area than they already had. The single purpose in them was to get and hold all the areas in him that they could. In the end, they chose to allow the song to sing—a wise choice, since it was far stronger than they.

"Fly with the sork..."

He tensed again. "And see with his eyes," he found himself saying, almost singing. "...of the choice at the fork..." The fork? The waterpaths split here and made a fork. What was happening? Was...

the song...? And then doubt and distrust flooded through him. Was it directed at himself? A feeling he was not sure of passed briefly through the others, intensifying them. How could a song help him now? And yet, it seemed that...

He shook his head again. Too many thoughts. Thinking could distract a Hunter and cause him to become lifeless as the result of an enemy attacking. Thinking was not something he wanted to do—not something he needed to do right now. There was only one thought that could be in his mind now. There was only one single purpose. It had to be the foremost thing in his mind! Nothing else could take its place! Remember!

Why was he there? His friend! Yad! And anything that helped him do this would be welcomed, whether it had a memory in him or not. His Hunter instincts needed much more work, he could tell. They had not been used properly, it seemed, for some time. They would serve him now, though. For he wanted nothing more than to become focused and have the Hunt be profitable. And he purposed in his heart to make it so.

At first, there was only darkness. Then a picture began to form. It was a simple picture. It was a simple, single picture—with a simple, single purpose. It had no form at first, no name. There were no memories with which to compare it. But a new memory that is being formed may not have old ones to look at it for comparing. And so it was with this memory. It made its own residence as it grew larger, taking home where before there had been none. And as it did, it took on form, and then a name. The form and name were now familiar to Narn, to the Hunter—to Narn, the Hunter. It filled him uncontrollably, and he found himself gripping handsfull of the soft grass as the vision of Yad being hurled through the air filled him and rendered his eyes sightless, then left him in the darkness again.

"No! Not the darkness!!!"

But when one invites in anything that might assist him in completing a task, even if it violates the Lessons one has learned, one cannot choose what will and what will not come forth. And, so it was that Narn again found himself being filled with the darkness of the losses. However, he was not listening to the effect of the losses now, only to the strength of them. For the Hunter needed that strength to face the coming enemy.

His hands were tightly clenched and shaking, pulverizing the bits of green ripped from the ground. Narn opened his eyes. Or, rather, his eyes opened. They only saw what they needed to in order to make a good Hunt. The streams were now easily seen disappearing into the forest. He set his jaw, threw down the grass, and set off in the direction the sork had flown. He would follow the words. They seemed to be as strong in him now as were his Hunter instincts. Indeed, it may be that the instincts made the song seem even stronger. He pushed his way into the tangle of branches—

—and stumbled headlong into another clearing. He raised his head and shook the dirt from his face. He was looking through a cluster of tamernans across the clearing. It was dotted with trees, much like the ones in his own land rather than the meshed jungle through which he had just come. The stream continued on— and disappeared into the mist. The mist. He saw it now. It rose and hovered in the air some distance away, shimmering in the newborn light that found its way between the gnarled trees and tried to dance with the mist as it moved in the soft winds..

Narn stood slowly and brushed himself off. After a few moments' hesitation, he walked toward the mist. The soft cries of the tamernans faded behind him as some of their mist retreated from his entry, revealing the stream flowing silently into a pool. As he moved closer, the entire pool came into view and he stopped. His eyes alone moved over the scene. Something inside him whispered.

"...Of the stopping of cries..."

His hand went to his knife. But his fingers reminded him of its aged and weakened condition, and in one swift movement he had the bow off his shoulder and an arrow strung on it.

"...The mist..."

His body vibrated. He strained to hear—anything, to see— anything. His eyes were locked onto the far side of the pool. Its quietness shimmered at him. What was he feeling? Fear? Even so, he would gather strength from it and put it in its proper place. But...why would he sense fear here?

There was nothing there.

But there should be. Something. And there was not. And the lack of something could cause one to fear what was missing...or what might be there. But...was it really fear he was feeling? Fear was not something to which he was normally susceptible...

"...The mist still your fears..."

He shook his head and winced as a pain shot through it as though he had been hit with something very solid. Yet, there was nothing there. How could he feel pain if there was nothing there? What was missing? There was something...

Then came the change.

As the mist parted for him, a calmness enveloped him. It began in his fingertips and surged through him so rapidly he did not have time to think about it. It was just there. It filled the emptiness as though it was what had been missing. He cocked his head slightly and looked again at the pool. There was nothing there. He looked around the pool. Three was nothing there—there was no danger. The arrow and bow began to lower.

Another whisper approached him, but he shook himself violently all over. The buzzing began again and he shook mentally. How could the calmness be all over him and yet— The whisper remained subdued, almost like the sound of a wind toying with the tops of the trees. He continued to walk, trying to concentrate on each footstep.

There was nothing to fear here, no danger at all. The bow and arrow lowered even farther.

The whisper toyed with the treetops of his mind.

"The mist stills your fears..."

He stopped and his eyes went to the bow, which was shaking. He looked at his hands. They were shaking. There was something— He tried to remember. The bow. The special arrows...the special points...

"...stills your fears, while the night breathes her breath..."

No! Fears are good! Fears keep you aware, alive! He had been taught— Yad had taught— Yad!

Yad!! *"YAD!!!"*

He fought the calming that was filling him, pushing aside all that he was feeling. His fingers gripped the bow tighter, his teeth clenched.

The whisper continued, but he ignored it now, not needing to fight it. It was no longer necessary. Fighting stopped when the battle had been won. And it was so. It was merely a matter of finding out who had been victorious. He straightened and stared into the fading mist and spoke, though no sound came forth, the last line of the song.

"The Great One appears; bring She life, bring She death?"

In defiance of the calmness, the Hunter drew back the string as far as the bow would allow and, his entire body alert, aimed the arrow at the mist still floating by the pool. The fingers held fast the specially-spun string, the power there to go forth and defeat the mightiest of enemies. The arm added its strength to that of the fingers in the holding of the string and the bow. The arrow was carefully strung to the string, patiently awaiting its freedom to add its force to the battle and aid the Hunter in his encounter. There would soon come the signals to release the missile and the scene before and around him would tell the Hunter when this was to be. There would be no doubt. There would be no Confusion. A Hunter did not draw his bow with arrow without need to use it. So he waited.

And Confusion left, its purpose satisfied.

There came no sound, no movement.

His eyes alone moved across the mist. It was quiet.

But some things can speak without words, without sounds. Some things can tell us much without pictures...or, at least, without those to which we have grown accustomed. And sometimes, when it is something very special, a new way of telling comes about. Those who have ears to hear will learn, and perhaps live. Others will find lifelessness awaiting them.

His feet spoke to him first. His ears realized that they did not know what the feet knew, and they were not sure what to do about this. All they had been trained to do was listen, and that they did. But their search was in vain, for there was nothing to be heard.

Then his legs reverberated, and before the ears could be in wonderment about them as they had about the feet, the sound was suddenly all around him, a fierce abusive pounding of the ground, that echoed in the clearing.

In one far-off area, the mist parted.

And he saw.

In one fashion, It almost moved in a motion that was so slow every fiber could be ascertained, and yet Its speed presented It as nearly a blur. Each movement was a tribute to Its spectacular frame, one that had been Designed to true perfection. The hooves were tearing up the ground as It came, causing the vibrating first in the ground where he stood and then in the air around him, the dazzling body they carried pulsing with unquenchable power as each muscle moved in perfect harmony as though it were one with and drawing it strength from all of nature surrounding it. The gleaming silver cone atop Its head was lowered toward him and getting closer with deadly accuracy. Its eyes that once reflected the faded copper of the dying lightbreak now contained the full brilliance of the Sun, and they burned with a fierceness that paralleled that of the Hunter.

All this was absorbed by Narn in but a single heartbeat, for the charging horror, complete in Its magnificence and a tribute to Its Maker, was nearly upon him. There was no doubt as to why the stories had called Them the Great Ones.

* * * * *

"It is said the Great Ones were everywhere then, living among the people, even talking with them, each helping the other."

Narn listened as his Father continued his tale, rubbing his hands together before the fireplace.

* * * * *

The scene blurred, and Narn, the Hunter blinked away the water. Truth was Truth, and when faced with that upon which one had based his life, even the hurts and losses paled. Old Lessons were awakened from their false sleep induced by the darkness affirmations who, again caught totally unaware, tried, in their blackness, to stand in the way of the Lessons and memories which came forth. But the Light of the Lessons shone into the Blackness, and the Blackness understood it not. It had to fall away.

* * * * *

Narn shuddered slightly. "But They were beautiful! There was a time when They lived with us. They have never done you any harm."

Yad sighed and shook his head. "Narn, the Hunters know better. A more fierce beast has never existed. They stalked their victims ruthlessly—"

"No!!!"

* * * * *

This had happened before. The scene blurred. His hands began to shake. He blinked away the water that had returned unbidden. Despite the resounding explosions of each hoof as it struck the ground, the whispering made itself heard—again. Yes, he knew this part of the song very well, and the words came across his lips without his commanding them to do so.

"The Great One appears; bring She life, bring She death?"

The vision of Yad being savagely thrown through the air struggled to fill his mind again and formed a dissonance with the whisper.

* * * * *

Narn shuddered slightly. "But They were beautiful! There was a time when They lived with us. They have never done you any harm."

Yad sighed and shook his head. "Narn, the Hunters know better. A more fierce beast has never existed. They stalked their victims ruthlessly—"

"No!!!"

* * * * *

His body shuddered. The bowstring became less taught.

* * * * *

"It is said the Great Ones were everywhere then, living among the people, even talking with them, each helping the other."

* * * * *

The scene blurred again. He let go the efforts to blink away the water and left his eyes closed. He dropped the arrow and the bow at his side, then let them fall to the ground. The fingers were initially somewhat shocked by the action, as it had never before happened. But they were always obedient to the Man, doing as they had been Made. They knew that if they performed exactly as commanded, the Man would be taken care of, regardless of whether they understood the commands or not.

The words stuck in his throat as he tried to speak them. But when words must be said and the lips cannot work, the heart is very active.

"Yad, it cannot—it must not be.— " Truth must live. And the last words came the hardest. The struggle was not long, although it had originally begun before the Sun had been Given its light and would last for always. The struggle was not really all that difficult, but the strength to win it was what was hard to come by. Not that it took that much effort to find. It was just that it took extra heart to actually perform the task of beginning the seeking. However, once begun, it was done. And then, as the Truth was there to set him free, the words were there. And they were spoken into the non-silence from his silence. "You—were— wrong."

And with these words, a coldness that had carefully hidden itself in front of the Lessons from his Father cried out silently and left him; a Blackness that had carefully hidden itself before the loves that he had felt cried out silently, struggled again to reassert itself, then, failing, left him.

In that Moment, the air around him became chilled and it seemed that the light from the Sun dimmed where he was. But it came between heartbeats and was not truly seen with the eyes, so it went unheeded.

And he accepted.

He could hear the powerful breaths now as the Great One neared, creating a symphony between themselves and the massive hoof beats.

And he knew.

"Sing, Fabra, sing..."

The word formed in the depths of his memories—it felt like that same place from which the song was coming. The word wound its way through him, past the once carefully-placed guards, for the dark areas were beginning to show their green of life again. The word came into his heart, then his mind, and his lungs opened to prepare to take in air to form the word—that would be his last word ever spoken—that it might be spoken out loud. And it became so.

"Fabra." The name came out choked across his lips.

XIV

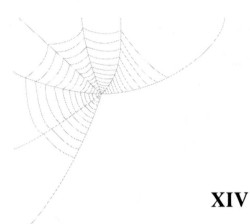

The sleeping fliers were shaken into startled flight and fled as the sound repeatedly reached them. The families of v'rill, startled from their sleep by the sound at such an early time before the light of the Sun touched their Home scampered about into the fields, searching for a new place to hide in their fright. This proved to be of little use, for the sound seemed to echo back again and again through the trees until it finally became soft enough to where it no longer could be heard by the ears. The trees that allowed and contained the echoes would go on hearing it for much longer. But they did not worry about running from it. There was little that frightened them. The wind that had first brought the dissonance returned along its path to where it had first found the alarming sound, and it blew silently outside the Home of Man.

The girl was sitting up in bed, her eyes opened wide in the first-light, her hands clasping the sleep cover to her breast, and her entire body shivering as the water ran from her eyes and forehead and the choked scream finally died on her lips.

Her Father and Mother burst into her room carrying their knife and spear. Seeing there was nothing, or no one, in the room, the Mother hurried to the girl's side and embraced her while the Father looked on, spear still in hand. He saw nothing at the window, and nothing had been moved in the room. A slight movement of his lips began as though he were not pleased with what had just happened. However, as quickly as it started to form it left, for the Father knew his daughter, and she feared little, was not given to useless dreams. Therefore, something serious had just happened. So he continued to look on, confident that he would learn what was causing such distress to the second greatest love in his life.

"Lua, Lua. What is it, child?" The voice of the Mother was soft, hushing as she held the girl and rocked her gently as she had when the girl had been very small.

Her voice was lost. Her breaths came in gasps. Her hands pulled at her hair and tied it tightly about her face and she shook her head back and forth. Every new breath brought another new shiver to her, and she was soon shaking as though it were the coldest of the Cold Times with her fire gone out. The normal hue in her skin that radiated a beauty even in the dark was now less than that of a glowing new Moon. Her eyes held no sight, looking into nothing, as though they did not want to see. Water continued to pour forth from the sightless eyes and ran onto her clothes and onto her bed.

"Lua." Her Mother's voice was louder now, concern rising. "Lua, child, tell me what it is. What has happened to you?"

She swallowed—and choked. Then, as she regained her breath, she cried aloud and buried her face into her Mother's shoulder. "I—I saw him!" she wailed. "I—**saw** him! Narn!! His Name—... His Name—has been Called!!!" And her words and cries became lost in each other once more.

The Mother inhaled slightly, looked up into the eyes of the Father, who was already looking into hers, and then both Parents closed their eyes together.

XV

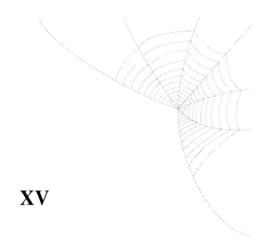

Silence was all around him. It was through him. It was a part of him. One may learn from other things that make noise, but many things can be gleaned from silence. One may know what it is like not to be heard. One may know of the silence of others. One may also learn from the ending of the silence. He had waited for always for the silence to end. And now he waited still.

But all things end. And waiting must also cease. For waiting to be suspended, something else must replace it. It may depend upon what one has learned during the silence as to what replaces the silence and the waiting. It may be that when they are gone, one may wish them to be returned due to the replacements.

He felt a cold chill run through him, although he could sense the warmth of the Sun peeking over the treetops. Therefore, he knew that what he was feeling regarding the heat or the cold had little to do with what was around him. So he would be able to ignore its effects and concentrate on something else around him. Breaths still came into and went out from him. All these things told him that he had not yet left the place of battle, even if the battle had been completed. He opened his eyes into tiny slits.

And he saw.

The Great One towered before him. The deadly cone was elevated high now and the large eyes looked deeply into his. The immense head then turned slightly and the eyes remained on him.

Narn forced himself to look at them—into them. It was not fear, he realized, that now caused him to have discomfort in looking at them. It was—an undefined feeling—one that seemed, somehow, familiar. He felt relaxation pour through him at the acceptance and with it, waves of fatigue flowed through his limbs. The earth tugged at him, and every sensation of tiredness, hunger, and thirst called out to him at the same time. He resisted. The thought briefly came to him that there might be something odd about facing the certain Calling of his Name and yet feeling such peace. But the thought was, indeed, brief, and, finding no home to nurture it, it left him as quickly as it had come.

The undefined feeling touched at him again. Uncertainty crept into him. This was not something with which he was familiar. To be sure, in the days of his youth he had encountered it, but he had seen many dances of the Sun and Moon since then... Its alikeness shook him and alertness returned. He watched as the unblinking eyes searched him from head to foot, the massive body unmoving save for the silent expanding of the sides when breathing took place. The Sun now reflected a deep copper in the eyes of the Great One. The fire, the intense burning, was—less. But there was not an absence. Something else was there. Something. Unnamed. Something that cried out to be named. The feeling. Unnamed. Yet—the eyes seemed to reach out. In exhaustion, he let it flow, unhindered.

And the feeling flowed.

It happened unexpectedly. He was not prepared. He could not have been prepared. Even the Hunter would have had no preparation. All that he had ever learned, all that he had ever seen, all that he had ever been taught, all that he had ever felt, all that he had ever known was in him and it came to life. The Lessons of his Father now filled his heart and all words of all others faded, diminished, fled. And when all things are as they were Intended, then there can be, again, one single Purpose.

And he *Saw* .

* * * * *

The Little One is sitting with Its Mother by the Pool. The twin Moons reflect in the quiet waters. Love is felt and nutriment is full.

Something moves on the other side of the Pool. Fear is felt. There is a noise. A strange beast rises. Desire to protect Its Mother floods through Its being and It charges.

Long before It rounds the Pool's edges, the Mother is standing and calling to It. It halts, confused. It must protect. But if the Mother calls, It must obey. Perhaps the Mother sees that the beast has been sufficiently frightened and She wants It back by Her side. It returns as bidden. When It looks back, the beast is gone and They are alone—and safe. The Little One feels pride.

The Mother nestles the Little One with Her nose.

Love is felt.

And the Mother sings to the Little One.

"Sing, Fabra, sing, for tomorrow will come

"When freedom shall ring where the Semsa is from.

"Fly with the sork and see with his eyes

"Of the choice at the fork and the stopping of cries.

"The mist stills your fears, while the night breathes her breath.

"The Great One appears; bring She life, bring She death?"

The Little One is listening to Her Mother. They are lying under a tree with huge blue blossoms. A single Moon is brilliantly shining overhead. Shadows dance as the blossoms move in the wind that plays in the trees. A story is being told. It is about how the Valley used to once be only a valley. Great Ones lived everywhere with Man, and they all lived together in harmony. And there was a special relationship between the Man and the Maker.

The Little One is playing in a field of flowers with another Little One that is running at the groupings of flowers and dashing through them with the small, but perfect, cone atop His head. The first Little One looks on. Sadness is felt. The other Little One is wishing the flowers were a herd of men. The first Little One feels more sadness, wishing Her friend knew about Men what She knew.

It is almost lightbreak, and the Great One is searching the forest for Her friend. The deep hoof prints lead toward the Clearing-By-The-Pools.

An emotion fills Her, one that is new. Normally, She enjoys the newness of things, but this feeling is not one that leaves Her comfortable. Discomfort is felt, although the source is unseen. She looks into the sky, but there is no danger there. She listens deeply into the thick growth around Her, but there is no danger there. And yet, there is something... Then a familiar feeling fills Her. It, too, is not one that leaves Her comfortable. It is known, but it is not well-known. It is fear. Not an ordinary fear, for fear can be used to strengthen. But this fear... This alarm...

The Great One begins to gallop as She moves through the growth. Trees give way to Her immense frame as She pushes through them as though they are but tall grass. Far in Her advance other animals are warned by the clamor She creates. The hooves... Suddenly She halts and becomes rigid. The green mist all around Her is not the same. The Sun has not yet touched it, and yet it is changing. Why does it change??

The mist does not respond to the questions of the Great One. It is only performing as it was Made to perform. It has been Told to change, and thus it does so.

As the Great One's eyes behold and the dread mounts within Her to a point of near-terror, the color of the mist alters and becomes the color of Her own skin. She sways a moment, the ground seeming to become unsteady beneath Her for a moment— She tries to deny what She has been taught about the changing colors— Then emotion fills Her anew and She charges off again into the mists which part for Her. Her powerful hooves dash the water from the waterpath, leaving a drying ditch behind Her. Her heart beats faster, sending more life into the legs and hooves that are now sending their signal throughout the Valley, smashing anything that is in front of Her as She moves on. Seeing becomes difficult. The bushes and trees before Her become blended into a single pulsating mass of greenery. It is as though Her seeing is being done through a veil of water. The great head shakes and the veil is removed—but only for a moment, for it returns. The head shakes again fiercely to remove the water again, feeling the anger well up within Her at its return.

Moments later, the last of the trees part for Her as She plummets into a clearing and gropes again for renewed strength finally coming to a halt as quickly as she had come into the clearing. The eyes do not want to allow their sight to gaze downward, but something pulls at them, commanding them to seek fulfillment of the suspected horror which is before them. The tower of beauty is standing over the body of another Great One. The magnificent lifeless frame is lying in a grove of crushed tamernan flowers. Earth and turf have been torn loose with the violent movements of imposed lifelessness in His final moment. His colorless eyes stare blindly into the discolored mist now being sung by the flowers. And protruding from His head, near His cone, is the shaft of an arrow of Man.

Rage. Horror. Bewilderment.

Hurt. A deep hurt, as though a part of Her has been destroyed.

She throws Her front hooves into the air and pounds at it. They are not the same when they reach the ground. They belong to a Great One Who feels determination and rage, all Lessons having been pushed deeply into hiding by the fierceness of these new passions. These are all new experiences for the Great One, and they go to the proper place within Her, that they may make demands upon Her later.

She crashes through the thicket wall, uprooting part of it. And then She sees the crumpled hulk of the Man lying beside his bow. His chest has been torn open and the ground all around him is stained in the deep red of the life fluids that drained from his body..

She can do nothing now. The slayer of Her friend is also lifeless. It is not enough! She has been deprived of that fulfillment! The fury indwelling itself deeper every moment She looks on, fills Her mind and cries out for vengeance! The hurt drowns out the Lessons She has received. She will have Her revenge!

* * * * *

Water filled Narn's eyes and overflowed onto his cheeks and down his face. He allowed it to fall now, unhindered, as though it were speaking about something whose words his lips could not find the proper words.

The large copper eyes were regarding him.

Narn felt as though a part of him had been destroyed as he looked back. His mouth moved but no words came out, choked off at the lump in his throat. He felt a shame enter him that one of his own kind had brought about this waste, but he knew that it was not one of his kind with whom he felt as Family. Even as such a close friend, this Man had made the wrong choice because he had listened to the wrong

Lessons. Narn could not undo what his friend had done. But...there was such...great loss here. If only he could do something. Such a One should not have to undergo such torture, such pain. If he could just help... If he could just reach out and touch Her...

He reached out. The Great One wavered slightly, muscles rippled, but did not move otherwise. He drew closer, looking up into the deep eyes, put his hand gently against the muscular leg and...—

An unnamed feeling became named. Truth lived again.

—*...Touched.*

Darkness became Light. Hate went away and love lived in its place. Anger cowered and crawled away and acceptance came into the void left behind it. And release came into the fibers of the creature where had dwelt all the poisons placed and left there from the feelings that had taken possession of them.

Narn's voice returned. It was the voice of one who had *Seen* and *Knew* . And he spoke softly what he knew. "Fabra."

The Great One quivered visibly all over. Her ears recognized Her name, even if it was being spoken in another tongue, and She had not heard the tongue of Man for many, many dances between the Sun and the Moon. She felt her heart begin to beat faster as her memory retold again of the time by the Pool when a Man had appeared. There was no doubt in Her, although She did not know how such things could be—that was for the Maker to Decide. She knew that this was the Man that had been at the Pool when She was a Young One. And now here he was again, sparing Her life and offering his. Lessons flowed now from their hiding places in Her memory; and recognition suddenly flooded its way into Her. She inhaled deeply, then exhaled as deeply and bowed low until Her cone touched the ground, the eyes following Her point. Other memories, much older, came forth. From the old days, the days of the Ancients, the feelings formed into thoughts, and then balked. The old language was all but forgotten. Indeed, it had been a long time. But some things...the good thing... remain. Thoughts raced, searching—and were rewarded. She gave forth a sound, a word—the word— the only word She now remembered. It had been unused for countless time periods, but it was said with a gentleness, almost a caress, and was held, even now, in the reverence it deserved. The voice was very low, but it carried its own echo as the calling of one distant flier to another and return. And it was almost sung.

"Semsa."

Narn tilted his head slightly and stood back a pace, not thinking about the fact that She had just spoken to him, but thinking about what She had said. "Semsa?"

The Great One rose and stood towering before him. Her eyes looked down into his, yet the spirit they radiated seemed to be looking up to him. And they smiled at him.

A smile raced faintly across his lips. He pushed his hair back. "Fabra? I—a Semsa?"

The Great One shifted from hoof to hoof, then looked around and up toward the jagged edges on the bordering mountains, and then back at Narn. "Semsa." Again the word came out in music, this time with ease, as She nodded Her head almost fiercely, Her mane waving around Her neck. In one movement, the cone was touching low again to the ground, then the head raised and the eyes were looking into his. And something was there that was shared between them. Then in a blur of iridescent near-white...—topin, She was disappearing now soundlessly into the remnants of the mist.

When the mist had completely burned off, Narn was alone in the field with not so much of an echo of the giant hoof beats left to hear. He sighed and let his thoughts relax and wander. It took no effort to do this. It happened without thinking. For when all things are as they are Intended, it goes much easier.

He thought of Yad. The vision of lifelessness and destruction was gone now. It would remain so. The old Lessons were alive again. He was free to feel what he had before. Truth lived, and the knowledge of that Truth had set him free. The fondness reached across time and would remain. His eyes looked knowingly across the expanse, and this time the words came forth effortlessly. "You were wrong, Yad. I will miss you, and I will carry what I have learned until I am Called back into the hands of the Maker."

His thoughts wandered again. There was much to think about now that he knew the Truth and was set free. From within, from the special place so Made, came the memory unthought-of, uncalled upon since he had begun his Journey. And, again, there was one single purpose, one single picture. The Village.

And he *Saw* .

Lua.

The steps of the girl were slow, dull, listless. They were coming from a place where there was no life. They were going with no life to a place of no life to do a task, but they were going nowhere. It mattered not. They would go as they had always gone, and they would return as they had always returned. But there was no longer purpose in them. There was no purpose for them. They merely were waiting for the time when they would no longer go to a place, a time when their owner would no longer give them instructions to do. They had accepted what was left for them and their owner. Nothing. They noticed not when they stepped on something in the way, nor if they actually went off the way. It mattered not if they were where they were going. There was nothing there for them—or their owner. They were an extension of her. She had nothing. So, they had nothing. And, in turn, they could offer her nothing. They—

A sork flew overhead, seeking v'rill for the meal for its family, unaware of the lifelessness going on below it. The v'rill ran into the cover of the thick brush to hide from the sork, unaware of the lifelessness going on near it. In a distant field, walking slowly toward its watering place, a huge togrun moved through the tall brush, its feet leaving tracks that could be easily followed—not that it feared. It had outwitted, outrun the Hunters before and would continue to do so. It was also unaware of the struggle of lifelessness going on a short distance away.

The scene before the girl was one she had seen too many times before on the walk to the stream, only now it was empty. There was the small pile of stones near the turn in the pathway, but there was no one to see them with her. There was the grove of trees where she used to hide and spring out to try and surprise—his name of life would not come into her memory of lifelessness—with his silly games. There were...

There was no change. All things remained the same. Yet, the scene changed. It was still the same terrain, but... Something had happened. The wind was suddenly warm now, the flowers again carried their delicious smell. She looked around slowly. She was alone. No one had spoken to her. Yet, something—someone... Her eyes jumped to the sky where the clouds were playing their drawing games with the high winds. How long had it been since she had seen... What was... It was becoming... She looked back at the path now, and memories as fresh as if they had just happened filled her with what it had been like to walk with...

The bushel of clothes fell from her grasp, her hands clasped to her mouth as she dropped slowly to her knees. Tears flowed freely from her eyes and she could no longer see the stream where she had come to wash. But that no longer mattered. She was sobbing, her breaths coming in gasps as her heart tried to keep pace with itself in the rekindling of a fire that had been allowed to go out. The words bubbled in happiness and uninhibited joy from her lips in the knowing. "Narn—my Narn! You are alive!! You are coming—back!!!"

Narn smiled as he gazed at the groping peaks of the rim. They presented a formidable barrier, a good protection for the Valley. But, he got in; he would get out. Tomorrow had come, freedom was ringing, and the Semsa was now again here. The tamernans would sing their color for Lua and him, and their hearts would beat together for always.

Truth was living.

It had been worthwhile.

HERE ENDS BOOK ONE OF THE NARN SERIES

CPSIA information can be obtained at www.ICGtesting.com
Printed in the USA
LVOW07s1113110913

351857LV00004B/46/P